PERMISSION

Pages 63–70 were first published in *New Writing* 6.1 (2009): 35–39.

Library of Congress Cataloging-in-Publication Data

Chrostowska, S. D. (Sylwia Dominika), 1975-
Permission / S.D. Chrostowska. -- First edition.
pages cm
ISBN 978-1-56478-858-0 (pbk. : acid-free paper)
1. Electronic mail messages--Fiction. 2. Epistolary fiction. I. Title.
PR9199.4.C4885P47 2013
813'.6--dc23
2013003455

Partially funded by a grant from the Illinois Arts Council,
a state agency.

Image Credits

Page 41: Obituary courtesy of *Gazeta Wyborcza*.

Page 54: *Anne and Margot Frank on the Zandvoort Seashore*, courtesy Anne Frank Fonds–
Basel/Anne Frank House/Getty Image.

Page 72: Peel, Paul, Canadian (1860–1892), *After the Bath*, 1980 (oil on canvas,
147.3 x 110.5 cm). ART GALLERY OF ONTARIO. Gift of the Government of Province of
Ontario. ©2010 AGO.

Page 77: ZOMO photograph courtesy of Wiesiek Bieliński.

Page 136: Burning church courtesy of *The Toronto Star*.

Page 139: Typical Stack Floor (fragment), Robarts Library. Plan from 10 March 1966. UTA,
Office of the Chief Librarian. A1969-0001 (19).

Page 161: Anderson, Alexander. Volume 1, p.34. *American engravings. 18--. Wood engraving.*
Print Collection, Miriam and Ira D. Wallach Division of Art, Prints and Photographs,
The New York Public Library, Astor, Lenox and Tilden Foundations.

www.dalkeyarchive.com

PERMISSION

S. D. CHROSTOWSKA

DALKEY ARCHIVE PRESS
CHAMPAIGN / LONDON / DUBLIN

To J. G. z. L. z. G.

N. Here's your manuscript. I have read it all the way through.
R. All the way through? I see: you expect few will do the same?
N. *Vel duo, vel nemo.*
R. *Turpe et miserabile.* But I want a straightforward judgment.
N. I dare not.
R. You have dared everything with that single word. Explain yourself.
N. My judgment depends on the answer you are going to give me. Is this correspondence real, or is it a fiction?
R. I don't see that it matters. To say whether a Book is good or bad, how does it matter how it came to be written?

N. But surely it's no more than a fiction?
R. Suppose it is.
N. In that case, I've never seen such a bad piece of work. These Letters are no Letters; this Novel is no Novel; the characters are people from the other world.

R. Your judgment is harsh; the Public's is bound to be even harsher. Without calling it unjust, I would like to tell you in turn the way I see these Letters . . .
   In seclusion, one has other ways of seeing and feeling than in involvement with the world; the passions differently modified also have different expressions; the imagination, constantly encountering the same objects, is more vividly affected by them. That small number of images keeps returning, mixes with all these notions, and lends them the odd and repetitious turn one notices in the conversation of Solitary Folk. Does it then follow that their language is highly forceful? Not at all; it is merely extraordinary. It is only in the world that one learns to speak forcefully . . . Passion, overflowing, expresses itself more effusively than forcefully. It does not even think of being persuasive; it does not suspect that anyone may question it.

Let me return to our letters. If you read them as the work of an Author who wishes to please, or who has pretensions of writing, they are detestable. But take them for what they are, and judge them according to their kind.

Jean-Jacques Rousseau,
Second Preface to *Julie, Or the New Heloise*

Let this be a short introduction. He received the first message, an email, one evening in mid-July. A week of silence followed and he received another, then another one week later, and so forth, quite regularly until the end of April of the next year. And as the messages became more involved, that measured intermission must have seemed too short to him. Though this may be construed as a selfish reaction, I suspect he saw the pace imposed by the sender as mechanical, even sadistic. The writer of these messages may have appeared over-reliant on regularity, not merely very disciplined but totally obsessed with discipline; then again, perhaps there was no inner compulsion; or perhaps the author wanted to appear exemplary, consistent and determined in his eyes, to give their work and effort more credibility, reality . . . In any case, even the said recipient's acceptance of these text-offerings, engaged without a word of reply, must have placed increasing demands on his time, which he might have liked to give freely, were that possible. What with his work schedule, travel, and other pressing business, he often could not reflect on them and, as another week elapsed, was mentally unprepared to receive more. Reading and rereading these "notes" required more of him than he could give, and more time than was at his disposal. One imagines also that initially he was too put off by their intellectual arrogance and posturing to have genuine interest in them. But as the communication became more erratic, his curiosity may have grown and eventually reached a point where it could scarcely be contained. On the one hand, the thorough reading for which he could not make time but now and then was compelled to, on the other hand, his increasingly cursory attention (immersed as he was in his own work)—such vacillation between the peculiar strangeness and pleasure of this reading and its absolute irrelevance to his life and work might have repeatedly led to frustration, so much so, he might have considered writing the author to ask them to let up, to allow him to catch up. But before he could bring himself to do it, he realized no doubt the relative minority of these events, or feared the encouragement a reply might give, or saw the tactlessness of such a request, contravening the correspondence's one-

sidedness, and understood that among the consequences of interrupting the flow and tempo of the writing was no less than its cessation. In the end, he honored the author's wish and never wrote back.

May 2008

Permission

(07.21.07)

Permit me to write to you today, beyond today. Not a letter, journal entry, or essay, much less a monologue or poem, but a note, and no more than *this note*—which, even if now it stands alone and autonomous, must now contain itself and attend to its own completion, aspires also, from the very first, to be more than itself, already knows itself as a fragment of some past or future whole: possibly of a book, making this an experiment in the writing of a book (that it is the opening of one is not out of the question), a book-ward writing perpetuated through *one* reader's reading of it, the writing and reading pursuant to desire and terminating at desire's end. Unquestionably and above all, however, this note is a gift, *an experiment in giving*.

That is to say, I want nothing in return, nothing tangible—*only permission to continue this spectral writing, so disembodied and out of place, so easily disavowed.* It is enough for me if your eyes follow this specter until it vanishes. I do not ask that you acknowledge me. You offered your work to the world with the hope it would set aside time for it, the time needed, and if indeed time was set aside for it in every time zone, if I set aside for it my own time, it was not on condition of reciprocity. If I now offer *my* work (a work in progress) to *you* (you of all people), it is with the same hope: that you too will set aside your time, the time needed for it.

You were not a random choice. My own identity, on the other hand, is random and immaterial. I imagine many strangers send you missives of gratitude as well as criticism, words beautiful and honest, bristling or brimming with emotion. Mine is one among those you randomly chose to open. My identity would mean nothing to you because we have never met. Revealing it alone would give nothing away and neither compromise nor raise *me* in your esteem. It would be of no consequence to your life since I as such cannot materialize in it. I prefer my fingerprints eroded by the anonymity of zeros, ones. Imagine this preference is for the sake of keeping honest an experiment that could break off at any point—without warning or explanation, without resumption.

Clandestine transgressions like this writing are easily forgotten, most of all by the perpetrators themselves. Because they are led to transgress against conventions by their desire, such people are unwilling to own up to its pursuit. They act irresponsibly to evade punishment by the *arbiters elegantiae*. There is no place for their adventure within the unbroken continuity of the everyday. Their activity must be kept secret if their desire is to continue burning with the same intensity. At once, certain inalienable elements of their pursuit end up sacrificed to this secrecy. The subtleties of reflection and emotion that made them take the boldest because decisive step—they are soon forgotten and cannot be retraced. I, for one, could no longer dramatize the conception of this writing. If confronted by common sense, I might admit its absolute absurdity. My avowal of this absurd act of writing would coincide with my disavowal of it. A well-kept secret can prove a trap for the weak of will.

But this absurd writing, its genesis lost in obscurity, must stand up to scrutiny. It owes a self-justification to its recipient, whose existence is central to it. This is because it belongs peripherally to a genre of writing perpetuated in one-one communication. Your attention, my *presumption* of your occasional attention, the attendant risk that what one *gives* might be *not received but discarded*—they are really this writing's epicenter. In effect, it behaves towards you like a moth does towards a flame (a chary moth, a cool flame); its ambivalence performs the conflict between two opposing forces (attraction, repulsion). It is drawn to the creation of meaning *à deux*, but resists the intimacy that would destroy it. It is a unilateral struggle for and against complete communion, much like a moth's dance around a source of light.

F. W.

(08.05.07)

I continue.

My previous note, the first, was really only that: the first note. All the same, a great venture; all the same, a mere introduction. I wrote *"this note"* to emphasize what it was: this note and nothing else, no more, no less (as yet); *this* note and not another, not the ulterior ones; this *note*, so not a letter, soliloquy, poem, etc.; in sum, *this note*, this preliminary and preparatory one, unlike the others that follow. I gestured at a continuation: I said (or said as much) that I will continue with your permission, prepared to accept silence, and accepting it finally, as tacit permission.

Since writing that first note, I have given more thought to my prospective work—this project I am throwing myself into with such abandon, (still) without surrendering myself to it, yielding no more of myself than necessary. I let out that first note to see if it would float—to test the waters with it, without trusting them myself—and it went fine, I hope, it did just fine on its own, untimely, unexpected, unprecedented, admitted, a bit suspect, opening itself to inspection.

I made no bones about my intentions: my note poised but already inclined windward, leaning into the wind, beyond the day of its arrival, towards the serious work ahead: the work to come. I gestured also towards a discontinuation, inevitable but unplanned, dependent on a writer's desire to write and on their reader's attention, meaning, of course, your attention. Although as yet I see no end to the work in sight, an end is bound to appear on the horizon, where thus far no dry land was seen, but only leagues and leagues of water: lulling the hull, washing over this vessel (my words) and its cargo (my meanings)—or the other way around: the cargo (my words) and its vessel (my meaning)—it is impossible to say *which* way with all this liquidity about, no solidity in sight. Objectively, this cargo is nothing but rot, cobwebs and rust; objectively, here comes not a trade ship but a ghost ship, its rigging in shreds; objectively, the coming book is a Flying Dutchman, surging *against* the wind, blowing forty knots *against* the water, no terra firma as far as the eye can see.

Like your work, once it is made whole this writing will be all-at-once. But will it ever be wholly complete—or will it end up suspended, even deliberately discontinued? A *stuttering, piecemeal, plotless* kind of work, not to be let out all at once: the metabolic course of a life, the traffic of unrelated thoughts and feelings, means continual delays and collisions, wrong turns and u-turns in the navigation of a work given one stretch at a time. A *serialized* work (as in the old days, when hacks could remain hacks and Balzac and Dickens could become Balzac and Dickens), one part detachable from the next and from the whole. The installments in anticipation of their installation in the whole, as a whole (the book); the writing an offering of book-ward fragments that ultimately dissolves the work (the whole). The whole easily reducible, its parts, in the end, adding up to less than their meager sum. The fragments attracted to yet resisting the coherent system (narrative, theoretical, philosophical). Steadily dissolving in discursiveness. Ending up beyond letters and belles-lettres. There is no turning point where creation (construction) ends and destruction (deconstruction) begins, when a breakthrough becomes a breakdown, when it is suddenly apparent that the present work (the writing of the book) means the permanent absence of the work (the book). Instead of the flow and ebb of a tide, a constant *undertow*, the heaving of a dark ocean.

Once I get over my aversion to repeat words in close proximity, in the closest proximity, where they already virtually overlap, where their cadences stumble into one another, their syllables echo each other, the tones of one word or phrase bleed into those of an adjacent word or phrase, and every repetition is embedded deeply in the rest; once, I say, I get over my inhibition to repeat the same words often, and often in the same sentence, I will have achieved what, in advance, I can confidently call a breakthrough in my writing. A breakthrough I owe to no one in particular, although one or two writers in particular convinced me of the uselessness, the unwieldiness, for a writer who has not yet had his or her breakthrough, of laboring under such inhibitions. The expression "to drag one's feet" is very apt for such a writer, on whom the weight of his or her inhibition is beginning to wear and its onerousness beginning to dawn; in every sentence or paragraph, everywhere in fact, you can see his or her reluctance to let go. This reluctance immediately makes me think, even think out loud, *second-rate*. There is a taboo on repetition, and consequently a fear associated with repetition, which both need to be challenged and overcome. The effects of such fear—not an incapacitating fear, rather, a *disquiet* associated with potential transgression, with making certain *offensive concessions* to what just may (or may not at all) be a creative breakthrough (but a creative stalemate)—these effects on a writer or artist can only be *salutary*. The mistaken notion that the greatest work and truth issue from fearlessness is really designed to keep in check those who *would dare* (if the formula were different) rather than be paralyzed by fear. The *fearless* work, from start to finish, is really a *running in place*, whereby no new territory is discovered, where nothing is ventured, nothing hazarded. Categorically speaking, nothing approached fearlessly is even worthwhile (I say). To be sure, the ancient Greek practice of *parrēsia*, of fearless speech—not merely verbal freedom but self-exposure in truth-telling in the truest sense—is far from worthless. But parrēsia, this candid, uninhibited speech, crowned the overcoming of (one's) fear, and I am all for it: awareness and overcoming of (one's) hypocrisy, (one's) conformism, for the sake of some important truth and personal probity, whatever the cost, no matter what risks involved. Repetition, then, might turn me into a petty outlaw but win me a little creative freedom. Even if I do not immediately stand to gain from it, I nonetheless swear by its discreet geometry. You are no less of a "desperado" for having broken through in your line of work, not least with repetition. Repetition, persistence, humanity! (origin, sabbath, divinity . . .). Repetition: a way of bringing into correspondence the obscurity of language, any language, and the clarity of things (put thus by Blanchot the Obscure).

Expect, then, an *incantatory* work—incantatory because of certain repetition, repetition of a certain kind (rhapsodic? harrowing?). A repetition akin to fire that has much to do with fire. The fire within the moth is like the fire without, which burns it up: both are the same fire. They blaze as they consume, and die when they have consumed.

Perhaps, however, there is no breakthrough, no advance. Perhaps *breakthrough* and *advance* are so different that there was no advance, only a breakthrough. Perhaps the entire *conceit* (this so-called note-making and note-mailing, the incessant, expectant writing) is bound to fall shy of expectations, to fall away from its first principles, to fall through. Perhaps these notes (one, two) are after all *less-than-notes*: mere oddments of thought, ramblings on to nowhere. Perhaps they are the germs of a book, perhaps of a disease. Sometime in the future I intend to reorder and edit these scraps to see if they be worth more than kindling for a fire. (The odd one might be worth something; the even ones are all kindling.) Assuming they are: what will have *come to fruition* will have been assumed as *germinal* from the get-go. Somebody will approach these odds and ends, my handiwork, and say, "The seeds of success were sown in the very first lines." Someone else will come along, nod, declare, "*Here* the creative act began," then, pointing to the other end, "*there* it ended." Regressions ad infinitum (to the artistic preconscious, the prehistory of the work, etc.) strictly forbidden! Definite appraisals from start to finish ("labor of love," "progress by leaps and bounds," etc.) strictly permitted! But precisely when the *creativity expert* pronounces "labor of love," I would intone "labor of hate." Precisely where he or she would have things end, I myself would have them upended.

Expertise (or what passes for it) will do in any work. Deleuze proposed that the secret of creativity is doing away with judgment. "Judgment prevents the emergence of any new mode of existence . . . If it is so disgusting to judge," he wrote, "it is not because everything is of equal value, but on the contrary because what has value can be made or distinguished only by defying judgment. What expert judgment, in art, could ever bear on the work to come?" ["To Have Done with Judgment"]. The question begs a response: not only do expert judgments bear on the work to come, they often also overbear the coming work. An artist, especially an artist wary of intimidating him or herself with premature judgment, has a hard time heeding such advice. He (or she) cannot help mimicking the expert, cannot but judge the work at hand, live in fear of that judgment, and naturally destroy (perhaps) their best work in advance. They are rare artists who can help themselves. Deleuze's advice to them is to obey only two forces: sympathy for things and antipathy towards things. But I envy the man who can put this advice into practice and be done with judging his (or her) non- or semi-existent work. To offer artists a piece of counter-advice: if you must judge, do so on *crooked* principles. It may be that the secret of creation is *secrecy* itself. If done in secret *until perfected* (according to one's own crooked judgment), the work might be deemed dangerous when revealed, but such a vague and offhand accusation will put it out of a judge's reach and within reach of a jury perpetually *out*.

Some see human life as one continuous act of creation, from start to finish, and all our actions as the result of a *creative force*. Artistic gift and genius may stand for uncommon degrees of awareness: of the beauty in everyday life and of time, braiding together remembrance, attentiveness, anticipation. But let creativity itself, they insist, be a *fact* of everyday life! Give it back to the hoi polloi! Only when one thinks of it as universal and *inescapable* in this sense does creativity become loathsome. Reduced to this vitalistic sense, it becomes the *condition* of a conscious relation to the world—even if we want none of this consciousness, and nothing to do with this world. Had I to choose between this *all* or nothing, I would rather creation were left to God.

F. W.

(08.12.07)

In Judaeo-Christian theology, divine creation, the work of His unimpeded will, is a *creatio ex nihilo*. Secular lore reserves the name of *genius* for the human equivalent of such creation. Genius is so exponential a growth of a man's creative power that he appears to have sprung out of the Godhead and pulled his works out of nothingness. It leaves everyone dumbfounded and fumbling for an explanation, unable to expose it as legerdemain. The man endowed with it is endowed with a will that overcomes setbacks to the realization of his creative potential. The greater his impediment, the greater is his overcoming, the greater his genius.

Though many aspire to it, most never touch the threshold of genius and pale in comparison to it. They seem fixated on creation out of nothing rather than out of something, and on creation unto something rather than unto nothing—in other words, on creation beyond the limits of human ability. Too often, victims of "early promise," they imagine themselves creating when they are actually recreating, and when they come to realize this, mediocrity and despair get the better of them: they feel their work is naught (there they are right), for they think creation must be of something absolutely original and permanent—a monument to creative power. Pretences aside, the modern secular cult of creative genius as a *divine gift* is *neither about really taking, nor about really giving, but about keeping.* If nothing is taken (since genius creates out of nothing) then nothing is owed. In fact, to keep his gift, a genius cannot fully give away his work; intellectually and nominally it remains his; and if he happens to disavow a work of his, he also doesn't give it away, for it then ceases to be the work of genius; and if he disavows all his works, and is believed, then he never was a genius, and loses his right to genius; and if he's not believed, then (though he betrays his genius) he becomes even more of a genius. Neither can he keep his work all to himself, since it is in return for showing and selling it that he receives the title of genius and collects its rewards. He keeps the rights to his works and does not share—much less give away—his genius.

As for me, I have always disdained the artificial self-aggrandizement that is so much a part of modern genius. Like others before me, I came to associate true genius with self-sacrifice, with betrayal of the whole damn myth of genius. I like to think of creating as *giving* more than anything else. I no longer think creativity a given, as those who hold the charitable (and lax) view that human life is immanently creative, that we are all gifted, as we are all creatures of God. But what would I call this *other* genius, which toils for nothing and gives everything away? What would I call such creation fully within the limits of human ability, which starts from something and ends in nothingness?

You may recall I designated my notes to you as "an experiment in giving." A sound experiment tests a hypothesis without guaranteeing its success. If it fails, one registers the failure. With just one experimental subject (not you, but me), this experiment of mine could not possibly be a controlled double-blind experiment. But a *double blindness*, nonetheless, plays a part in it. You can't see me: I stay behind a screen. I can't see you: your reactions, if any, remain invisible to me. My passion to write is evident to you, but not in plain view. Of the two sides of passion—*desire, suffering*—only one at a time can be turned towards you; the other (like the lunar dark side) is always in shadow. Being my own experimental subject, I am particularly prone to subjective bias in my observations. Even if I take care to correct it I will still have my blind spots.

The objective of this naïve natural experiment is to test the *gift hypothesis*, which runs as follows: *it is possible to give away one's creations without receiving anything tangible in return, or any other form of recognition or gratification. Moreover, such giving is possible and permissible within the Western conventions of giving (despite breaking with our economy of giving) without Indian giving.* My experimental question is thus: to what extent can I pour myself into a vacuum: devote mind and energy (which go into the creation of my gift) to communicating with your silence and possibly indifference, yet without *giving in* to silence and indifference myself? To "achieve" this one must let go of oneself, not merely to *give of* or *share* oneself, but, little by little, to *give oneself up*. I do not need myself to create and give, and naturally cannot hold on to myself when I give myself so wholly, even if I retain something of myself when I give myself *piece by piece, until the last* when I am no more.

What I am working out is an elementary philosophy of giving that is, by its very definition, *anti-Western*—that is, if one agrees that the West has neglected, and today lacks, an organic philosophy of giving, having only ever embraced a false metaphysics of giving (Charity), and, in the sciences, an inhuman notion of giving (the transfer and transformation of matter and energy), not to mention a sociology of giving. The founder of this sociology, Marcel Mauss, studied the anthropological history of the giving and receiving of gifts. He identified *reciprocity, solidarity, authority* as principles and products of gift-exchange among "archaic" societies operating on a gift-economy. He recognized in this a lesson from history. But if today the sky hangs low over global culture, where it is held that the money-economy and commodity-exchange have tarnished the apparent purity of this earlier form of social bond-formation, it is not because reciprocity, solidarity, authority as such have disappeared from the practice of giving. Oh no, reciprocity, solidarity, authority are still the main principles and products of giving. The *quid pro quo*, "something for something," is as central to the exchange of gifts as it is to the exchange of commodities. And even schoolchildren know that giving gifts wins friends and power, that selective solidarity benefits trade. Each type of exchange positively ensnares us in reciprocity, solidarity, authority.

What I want to measure—or, rather, what I want to obtain an impression of, since I do not claim exactitude of measurement for my results—is my own potential for *creatio ad nihilum* (creation fully within the limits of human ability, out of something and unto nothing). To rephrase my experimental question: can I give away what is inalienable from me (my utterance, myself) without the faintest expectation or hope of authority, solidarity, reciprocity? Can my giving be unhinged from a sense of both *investment* and *pointless expenditure*?

The relationship formed through such difficult and obscure giving (my writing) is not solid, and does not lead to solidarity. On the contrary, it is *solvent*, and leads, through its progressive dissolution, towards the final *solution* of this writing (my work), which meanwhile becomes progressively less difficult, less obscure.

The writing of a book, for one, is both blindness to the absence of the book and a vision of the book to come. This book must be envisioned as *present* in a dual sense. On the one hand, as being already here, even in the (present) process of its becoming, of its being written; its coming into existence and its eventual existence as a whole, its all-at-once-ness (in my mind's eye, and eventually in the eyes of its reader), are to be treated as givens. On the other hand, the book (whole) must be envisioned as *being given*, and eventually *given* as a whole; its writing is *given to being read*, it is *giving* oneself (the writer) to one's sole reader, and wholly *given over* once it is made whole by *having changed hands*. But the present work is also *compelled* to presence (by my unaccountable desire to write it) and suffers *forfeiture* (its loss in consequence of an offence or a breach of agreement). This writing remains, at least for its duration, a transgression of privacy and a breach of certain literary conventions. Your permission, a permission both tacit and after the fact (that first note), does not clear its name—even if it (this writing) is obsessed with clearing itself in your eyes, and may well *clear itself* in the end. Here is a curious case of the misdeed (the writing, the commitment of this work) being not merely identical but coincidental with the penalty, much as desire is sometimes equal to suffering.

So it goes: once this work is begun, once I begin giving myself up to this work, I cannot voluntarily or impulsively give up the writing. Eventually *the work itself* must conclude; even if one falls victim to an interminable writing obsession, exhaustion is sure to put an end to it sooner or later, so when the obsession starts up again it is already with another work. If one is pregnant with a work (a book), it must be given up—the precise moment of surrender is indeterminate, the process of its separation from the writer an organic process through and through. He or she may end up losing by it the right to write. The finished work, any finished work, is a ruthless, stubborn object, and frequently vicious. If, after much labor, it is born solid into the world, it may be only to bury the writer's name forever. That said, for a work to hold together, it cannot be given up prematurely, just as it cannot be given up past maturity. All effort must be made to deliver it at just the right time, as expected—an effort that is necessarily futile. And so it is virtually unavoidable that a work delivered whole, all at once, will be stillborn, and no amount of reading will revive it. But if the work is given life and given *piece by piece*, and the heartbeat of every piece is strong, then it lives (survives?) in *becoming* a work—even though it dies once it *has become* that work. This, too, is part of my experiment.

F. W.

(08.19.07)

One is not alone in identifying the moon with (human) *passion* and, conversely, the sun with (inhuman) *dispassion*. As regards the latter, you need only think of *Solaris*, through which Lem and then Tarkovskii expressed their horror of this sentient, egocentric star mutely exhuming man's unconscious memories. The dispassionate nature of the sun naturally lends itself to psychological ambivalence. The provocateur Bataille described our "human tendency to distinguish two suns" as follows:

> The sun, from the human point of view (in other words, as it is confused with the notion of noon) is the most *elevated* conception. It is also the most abstract object, since it is impossible to look at it fixedly at that time of day . . . In practice the scrutinized sun can be identified with a mental ejaculation, foam on the lips, and an epileptic crisis. In the same way that the preceding sun (the one not looked at) is perfectly beautiful, the one that is scrutinized can be considered horribly ugly . . . The myth of Icarus is particularly expressive from this point of view: it clearly splits the sun in two—the one that was shining at the moment of Icarus's elevation, and the one that melted the wax, causing failure and a screaming fall when Icarus got too close. ["Rotten Sun"]

The supreme and solitary indifference of the sun and its divine symbolism motivate its association with *genius and madness*. As Bataille notes, staring at the sun is a symptom of madness. The retina is branded with a negative sun: a black spot or hole corresponding to the blackened disk of the sun, which takes the place of vision and, hence, of understanding. Madness is indeed a mental blindness: excess of reason, overexposure to divine consciousness.

In his memoirs, Judge Schreber not only hallucinated two suns, one earthly, the other cosmic; he also *stared down* the sun, having it pale before his eyes. It was as if he were a light more potent than the glare of the sun or fancied himself in command of superior powers of consciousness. His auto-analytic zeal seems to suggest that the ocular fixation on the sun is really a *confrontation* with the sun (instead of a capitulation to it). In other words, a lunar influence, a sign of *lunacy*. The blotting out of the sun by sustained gazing is analogous to a solar eclipse. Our consciousness ("inner sun") is blocked by an impenetrable shadow, which temporarily obliterates all light. The moral implication of such profound darkness need not be a "dark night of the soul." Lunacy, after all, is insanity spasmodically relieved by clear-mindedness. Despite an insane passion, the lunatic maintains some control and *periodic* clarity of mind. In this the lunatic's lot differs from the madman's, who submits to the sun's commands (an extremely literal case of this Bataille recounts in his essay on Van Gogh). Lunacy is not total unreason, just as the moon is not everywhere the sun's opposite: it reflects the light emitted by the sun *as its own, dim light*, its reflective surface an interface between it and the sun. The lunatic *confrontation* (passion contra dispassion) is not a contradiction (passion over-against reason).

Everything that physically makes up the sun is subordinated to the garish rationality of its nuclear processes. The progressive cooling off of the sun further attests its dispassion. The ugly surface of the moon, meanwhile, is plainly the site of intense passion: the *maria*, depressions into which lava once flowed; the water found on it, tears; the impact craters, the scars of bombardment by comets and other cosmic bodies; the moon's dark side, a site of longing; the illuminated side, of suffering exposed by the sun's blaze.

Just as the sun has two faces—two affectless states (life and death) ruled by dispassion—so the moon, too, has its two aspects—the dark and the luminous—representing two affective states (desire and suffering) governed by passion. The affective peculiarity of the moon is that its lambent side (suffering) is really the darker, owing to its subdued and strange illumination, and that its dark side (desire) is less obscure for *not* being illuminated. One means this of course figuratively, since passion is obscure even (especially) when illuminated, since, like the moon, it is naturally dark—*potentially* illuminated by consciousness, by the so-called light of reason, but *actually* provoked by consciousness, becoming too obscure for reason. Consciousness, seeing itself as the object of such negativity and revolt, casts light on the mystery of the unconscious and its symptoms, but remains blind to its inner workings. Likewise, the lethal and life-giving sun, sublime in its nuclear perfection, lays bare only the surface imperfections of the moon, reveals the moon only as a curious *surface*, pitted and impotent, neither generating nor radiating its own energy, only borrowing it from the dispassionately generous sun.

An absurd figurative binary is thus established: that the sun *gives* and the moon *takes*—that (rational) dispassion only bestows and (irrational) passion only receives the muted light of reason. It is clearly entrenched in the alignment of these celestial bodies with activity (sun) and passivity (moon), strength (sun) and weakness (moon), and with the sexes in the act of copulation and reproduction. And it is this precise dichotomy, underpinning the Western practice of giving, that I dream of overturning. There is, first of all, nothing dispassionate about true giving, as there is nothing dispassionate about true receiving. Without passion there can be no *human* creation—no *creation-unto-nothingness*—which is the human form of giving, and so no true giving, the kind of giving that I am putting to the philosophical test, to see if it can be the basis for a philosophy of giving, which in our Western day and age is sorely lacking. Passion is essential to true human creation, thereby to true human destruction; it is equally well known that human dispassion (rigid moderation, abstract or instrumental reason) neither truly creates nor truly destroys—that is, creates or destroys by fulfilling the human capacity for creation or decreation. Take this writing: it is evidence of a writing passion turned discursive lunacy (instead of violent madness of reason); it confronts the selfishness of reason, the myth of genius, which shares ostentatiously but really gives away nothing of what it creates "out of nothing." It is a work of invisible fire: on the one hand, a fascination with the conflagration that is the sun, on the other, a revolt against the sun's egotistic brilliance.

The giving I am here putting into practice I could call "one-sided"—and mean this *one-sided* in a double and provisional sense. My gift is unilateral by coming solely from me. It is, moreover, a gift with only one side of passion illuminated in any given instance of giving. But in no time at all it has become apparent that this description ("one-sided") is doubly inadequate. After all, I am also *your* beneficiary: you inadvertently make me a gift of your silence, which permits me to give unconditionally, and *if* you follow this text (I do not always presume you do), I also gain from the benefit of your doubt. Your generosity of silence and doubt is no projection of my own generosity. Moreover, the light cast on one side of my passion—ever the passion of a writer for his or her writing—is cast unevenly, does not illuminate every area of this side with the same intensity. The areas of relative obscurity on the unevenly illuminated side of passion (suffering) evoke the other dark side of passion (desire), the one not illuminated. So you can see that *one-sidedness* is hardly accurate. By the same token, our *double blindness* is not so bereft of light.

F. W.

P.S. By titling your last film *Rabbit Hunt* you gave yourself away (Renoir, Bresson . . .). As farfetched as it may sound, the rabbit hunt stands for the lunacy of cinema—as the moth's dance does for the lunacy of writing.

P.P.S. How subtly Native American myths invert our Old World hierarchy of man, animal, and cosmos. A Micmac fable has it that a rabbit, who was himself a hunter, caught a moonbeam in one of his snares and, upon freeing the bright captive, almost lost his sight!

P.P.P.S. In the old days I used to feel less of a *writer*, now writing is becoming a distraction for me, like rabbit hunting for the cracked-brained. Were we to roll up our sleeves and "cut to the chase," the end of this predatory pursuit, this vain ambition, would be exhaustion and impotence. Would we do better to call off the dogs and let the great work be? Or does the effect of impotence precede the cause of evident ambition?

(08.26.07)

A few years back I applied myself briefly to a study of solitude. I abandoned it as soon as I sensed I could no longer fully inhabit the experience of solitude—that, at least for the foreseeable future, this experience was at odds with my unchosen lifestyle. Reviewing the notes I made at the time, I came across this fragment: "The truly solitary, despite or because of their solitude, harbor the desire for a mutual apotheosis with an ideal other or for the consummate surrender of themselves to this other. Their ideal counterpart is: a deity, a genius, a dead friend or kinsman, someone they once knew and won't know again, or someone they hope to meet and know in some future time, or in another lifetime." I owe a part of this none too profound thought to Montaigne's melancholy essay "Of Solitude." In it, he distinguishes the practice of solitude in active life from the mature solitude practicable in retirement. Neither species of solitude is, for Montaigne, strictly predicated on physical isolation, but both are "enjoyed more handily alone." The solitude of one's autumn years is largely a radicalization of its younger counterpart: we must remain true to ourselves and our imagination, but curb our desires and ambitions. We are urged to prepare "securely"—and this is "no small matter"—for our withdrawal from this world through death:

> Since God gives us leisure to make arrangements for moving out, let us make them; let us pack our bags; let us take an early leave of the company; let us break free from the violent clutches that engage us elsewhere and draw us away from ourselves. We must untie these bonds that are so powerful, and henceforth love this and that, but be wedded only to ourselves. That is to say, let the other things be ours, but not joined and glued to us so strongly that they cannot be detached without tearing off our skin and some part of our flesh as well. The greatest thing in the world is to know how to belong to oneself.

To attain such deathward solitude, we are advised as well to cultivate *imaginary fellowship*: to imagine ourselves in the company of great men. "[M]ake them controllers of all your intentions; if these intentions get off the track, your reverence for those men will set them right again. They will keep you in a fair way to be content with yourself, to borrow nothing except from yourself, to arrest your mind and fix it on definite and limited thoughts in which it may take pleasure . . ." To learn mature solitude we need the censorship of a strong conscience to remake us into someone in whose sight we would not dare to walk awry.

My solitary correspondence (this writing) cultivates something like this. It is the work of fellowship in solitude and of solitude in fellowship. Since I owe this solitude to *your* fellowship (fictive, to be sure), I cannot call it—any more than this writing—fully *mine*; I must also call it *your* solitude—and *your* writing. And, insofar as it is not entirely make-believe, my fellowship is anonymous and virtual; as is this solitude, I fear.

Worldly ambitions and the enjoyment of fame are antithetical to solitude. You give your life to light, being less and less content to lie (and wither) in the shade. But a quiet, secret ambition need not be contrary to seclusion. It can provide mental sustenance without distracting from higher ends. A hermit's pursuit of truth, provided the species of truth pursued is transcendental, is not at odds with ultimate solitude. "It seems reasonable," so Montaigne, "when a man talks of retiring from the world, that he should *set his gaze outside of it*." A focus on oneself, unless it is for the betterment of oneself in the eyes of a divine being, unless it is a self-abstracting sort of self-reflection (what is called *omphaloskepsis* or the contemplation of the *cogito*), is not conducive to, indeed detracts from, thoughts of transcendence. A focus on oneself as an end in itself, purely on account of one's selfhood, seeking therein one's profoundest desire, brooks no true satisfaction. Narcissism, whose flower is so reminiscent of the sun, is really the bane of solitude.

It is a moot point whether or not solitude is wholly devoid of passion. Strict definitions of solitude should be approached with caution. One may define solitude as being spiritually centered, free of desire and mental suffering, with thoughts devoted to the *vanitas vanitatum*, composed for the hereafter; but one's own solitary experience quickly points up the stifling narrowness of a definition that pledges one to sift through the silt of everyday experience for infinitesimal particles of gold: the exceedingly rare moments when nothing disrupts one's quietude, when one is easy about one's mortality, reconciled to every banality and evil (and beauty's associations with them), when one reins in one's sympathies, or, having settled accounts with the world, is prepared to part from it. By the time one adds to this definition the most commonsensical requirement—that of secluding oneself, of living alone and shunning all company—solitude becomes impossible. It mimics death, which may be a model for solitude, but an unlivable one. Although through such elimination we have indeed isolated something pure, the alloyed gold of lived experience reveals to us solitudes vastly more complex.

As far back as I can remember I felt at ease among the dead. I made a habit of frequenting cemeteries wherever in the world I happened to be. My fondest memories are of exploring the Old and the New Povozki in Warsaw, the churchyard of Peksovy Bzhyzek in Zakopane, Père-Lachaise in La Ville Lumière and the Glasgow Necropolis modeled on it, London's Highgate, burial grounds in the Irish Midlands, and the maze-like Montjuïc cemetery, whose scabrous crests overlook a topography of the port of Barcelona.

There have been countless others besides, of which I have no clear visual recollection because, in their comparatively lesser picturesqueness, they served me rather as spaces for melancholy reverie. Through my solitary appreciation of cemeteries, I became convinced that people who seek true solitude sooner or later wind up in a cemetery— and I reckon that those who stop at cemetery gates and walk away, as if abashed by where they find themselves, never do find true solitude ("some stones are better left unturned!"). The sense of having absented oneself from society is most palpable there, in a city of blind addresses and unseen inhabitants. That being said, in my traversing of graveyards, in my pursuit of solitude among the departed, I was in fact always after fellowship, and in my pursuit of fellowship always after solitude. But while before I thought solitude and fellowship irreconcilable, and my pursuit a temperamental inconsistency, I now see them as intertwined.

F. W.

(09.02.07)

Even if no one took note of it, I make note of it. A child viewing a child's corpse. One in black, fidgeting, the other in white, immobile. This *tableau mort* is a lesson in solitude.

The child alive in the arms of his father is my father. The dead child I don't know. Like someone who has never seen their own image and can barely recognize themselves, I initially miss our close resemblance. How I long to incarnate this beatific image of death.

Growing up in wartime, my father was no stranger to death. He knew it, one might say, intimately—not as a butcher or a mortician knows death, through the corpses he deals in, but as only a child daily witnessing the *event* of death could know it. Surely he knew what death meant: it meant you were out. You existed, but in the ground, with your own kind, and the living continued to care for you, betimes thought of you, or erased all memory of you. Being alive meant just the opposite: you participated, led your existence above ground, and the dead also continued to care for you, sometimes thought of you, or else consigned you to oblivion.

It is a photograph of existential equipoise. The living in it outnumber the dead, but the dead occupy the centre of the picture. The gazes of three individuals related through the sight of death: a woman of childbearing age (who is not my grandmother), a man, and a child seemingly belonging to this couple. The dead child apparently the younger sibling of the child still alive. The actual story I don't know. The event of death had been superseded by a corpse, a coffin bestrewn with flowers, a brilliant whiteness, the sunny frame of mourning.

F. W.

(09.09.07)

I have witnessed neither birth nor death. I consider it my handicap. It may be I instinctively removed myself from situations where either was in the offing by paying undue attention to fatal (as opposed to vital) signs. At the same time, if memory serves me, I had always been aware of death and magnetically drawn to organic remains. Memorable in this respect were the many summers spent on the rural property of my grandparents: a swamp forest, a gnarled orchard, a dirt yard with a well, a pre-war home. Reflected in a tall canted mirror, deer trophies jutted out from the walls of their cramped living room. Hooves, hides, and antlers transfigured themselves into ashtrays, rugs, and chandeliers. Outside, I had my hands full of bones and carcasses of dogs, cats, nutria, and sundry species of birds. One by one, my grandfather beheaded a dozen hens that I had raised in our apartment in the city (I remember a bloody tree stump and carmine sawdust). And as his patience wore thin, he also did away with his caged weasels and rabbits; left unattended, they would have been a nuisance. Unable to mourn all these fatalities, I took comfort in a daydream: that the handsome cockerel, which disappeared in a panic underneath a sideboard never to reappear, was a survivor. Yet even in wintertime hungry forest animals left bloodstained tracks in the snow narrating their cruel destinies. These mortal rhythms continued for a number of years and made on me an indelibly mournful impression. What else could explain why, at eight years of age, I traded my best toys for a stuffed pheasant, a creature of (I now recall) baroque magnificence. In hindsight, this apparent foible marked an aesthetic turn in my once indiscriminate fascination with what had perished.

Eventually my paternal grandfather and grandmother passed away, and the sliver of land they cultivated entered a period of still-life. I rarely had occasion to visit there. Then, aged seventeen, and shortly before arsonists torched the old village house, I began writing. The first story (without my realizing it at the time) was told by me as an adult: a man employed in a bookstore whose windows gave out onto a busy public square and were meaningful only as a vantage point. I cannot say whether this nameless book vendor was my ideal future self-image or a compromise with the realities ahead. I cannot return to the mental station in which the character was conceived, and so I cannot delineate his significance at the time. In retrospect, however, I feel that he was a product of signal lucidity of mind. I recall producing many versions of my future self premised on my seminal role in society, all of which were fantasies driven by ambition, at that time utterly groundless. So while I cannot indeed retrace the steps my unwitting younger self took to arrive at this alter ego—a solitary man behind a bookshop counter—I now feel the figure to be at once the most honest, selfless, and altogether the most tolerable in my repertoire. My concern with making meaningful life choices in pursuit of well-defined goals cast me naturally in the role of self-observer.

But there was more to the story, penned in earnest at that unripe age. The observer-narrator singles out one individual amid the undulating throng he watches in the square. It is anyhow a man whom no-one notices, who is even humbler than the book vendor, and whose casual occupation consists of handing out leaflets to passers-by. The narrator follows this man during his dinner break into a shaded corner of a nearby park. He watches the other sit on a bench and drink from a flask tucked in his pocket. He is older than me, notes the narrator; his addiction obscures his real age. Meanwhile, the stranger's eyes glaze over, sweat streams profusely down his temples, his head jerks back once, and body slumps over to one side. The narrator observes these signs as he stands washing his hands in a round, tiered fountain topped with a stone maiden holding a water jug. He has witnessed a cardiac arrest, and the rest of the story implies it was mortal. The man's legs are outstretched, one of his feet twisted slightly at the ankle. His bottle has slipped down into the grass. His wide-open eyes are motionless, rather like the glass eyes of stuffed animals—which lent the story its awkward title: "Człek wypchany," Stuffed Man. But it was likewise true that the bookseller had himself an empty head on his shoulders, what is called *an open mind*, and that, moreover, his observation was distinctly insensate.

But there was still more to the story. It begins, in fact, with a kind of dossier on the deceased. Stefan, for that is his name, is no reprobate. He is a sensitive, solitary soul with a drinking habit. He bonds with his pet turtles—among them *Pelodiscus sinensis*, whose eyes express unmistakably human sentiments—and is very fond of the lush flora taking over his rooms. We are given a description of this commodious family house, its degradation years in the making. But why paraphrase juvenilia, written long ago and advisably forgotten? My head, swimming from drink inside a noisy establishment, is momentarily stumped by the question.

Only after I gather up my change and shuffle outside do I hit upon the answer. Why, the narrator's encounter with his object—a predator-prey kind of encounter, there's no denying it—leads him to realize that his position as observer is no longer tenable. With mounting curiosity, enamored of his powers of perception, he unknowingly beholds what was meant for no other eyes but those now lifeless and turbid, already turned inwards. He himself remains unobserved. This ultimately *missed* encounter, the unrecognized snatch of death, the final repose whose sanctity his stare had hopelessly profaned, put him to shame. I see him (me) humbled as in the presence of a mendicant seer or holy fool. He (I) will be well served by it.

F. W.

(09.16.07)

He was my friend: a failed painter, who could have easily become an eminent painter, but instead wasted his creative energy in seeking accreditation from the Academy. For several years straight he tried to enter that stern institution, competing for a spot among "the best of them"—the ironies were not lost on anyone who knew of his disdain for the "Academy of Fine Arses" (the fair sex being there in the majority). He took pains to improve where there was no room for improvement, where he could only deteriorate (in our eyes he already ranked with the best of them). Even before gaining admission to said Academy one had to paint like its student, one had literally to be molded by it in advance; yes, to get into it, one had to already have gotten through it. A shining diploma and an artistic spirit were not enough to ensure success; one had, first and foremost, to reproduce the style of painting formally promoted by the Academy and forego all displays of artistic independence, including original interpretations of the Academy's style. One had to prove oneself *a natural* in this style, suitable for broken-spirited novices who worked years only to end up just where they began. For my friend Peter Vomela, beginning at the beginning was a serious hurdle, since he was far along the creative path already. He would not let himself be molded and toned down, even if he sincerely desired to satisfy his entrance examiners. With each attempt, the integrity and originality of his artistic statement must have stolen the show but also cost him a place in *the fold*, so that eventually he blew his chances at ever getting in and breaking down the ossified forms of the fine arts establishment. After years of thus wasting his talent and energy, years which need not have been wasted and which he did not otherwise waste, seeing as he applied himself casually to the study of art history at the Academy of Catholic Theology—during and after years of biding his time thus, reading and studying, not drawing or painting (not, that is, putting to use the techniques he read about and studied in art history books or developing his craft), his talent—which at that point must have been immense—suffered surely irreparable damage.

I remember vividly his *last stab at art*. I came home for the winter holidays and reconnected with friends I had known since grade school—children or grandchildren of intellectuals, diplomats, artists, aristocrats, some boasting foreign (Hungarian, German, British) roots—living in the Zholibozh district, which formerly, before the war, was the most refined of Warsaw's districts, the intelligentsia district, but during the war had been razed, and after the war partly built up, and which may yet be rebuilt in the old mould. I remember then being invited to a New Year's get-together at Vomela's house on Kossaka Street, a house I adored as a child, with its upper-class European décor, many empty rooms pending exploration, a wide, sunny veranda with a garden swing, and a basement that doubled as a rehabilitation facility, housing massage and exercise equipment and an indoor swimming pool. This subterranean dungeon—I could never resist thinking it a dungeon—was fitted out for his older brother, whose mental development stalled at the age of twelve when he dove from the second storey onto the wide veranda.

I remember Vomela as a rare bird even at an early age—we attended the same elementary school. Later, driven by curiosity, I began to appreciate his confirmed eccentricity, which was innocuous and could even be charismatic. He reminded me in so many ways of the writer-artist Witkacy. Although he had pretensions to the so-called artistic lifestyle, these, however, manifested themselves (more often than not) in polite and orthodox ways: gawky gestures, deliberately dated and neat attire, unstudied mannerisms and pundit impersonations which came easily to him, given he was the scion of intellectuals, moreover of German extraction. At that time I myself had no pretensions to creativity and was on a patently misanthropic course, swept up by the available forms of counter-cultural rebellion. I was also staunchly anti-artistic: I could not stand straight-faced aestheticism and urbane pastimes, I wanted no part in accepted avant-gardes. At the same time, you could not call me anti-creative—actually, I had a wealth of pent-up creativity, was so creatively *charged* that static sparks flew when I rubbed shoulders with creative types. Vomela's polite nonconformity and general decency could not therefore fail to impress me. I was always fumbling for myself and defining myself by this or that ferment of youth. He was always creating himself, never defined himself by any percolating movements. In all respects I took him for the real thing. He had me seduced by creative license, by outrageous ideas for leisure, by a gaze faintly salacious and lips obscenely put to use on women too unnerved to resist. When one observed him, as it were, in action, whether this was painting, conversation, or advances, his appearance and behavior were no less than enthralling. But when one found oneself, as I sometimes did, the object of his attention, then these same actions resembled verbal and physical assaults. Perhaps it was my own insecurity that turned our encounters and rare tête-à-têtes into *creativity matches*. We were never on a par; he outmatched me every time.

I have fond memories of spending several summer vacations with the two Peters, Vomela and Barbak, the three of us holed up in a whitewashed log cabin in the Subcarpathians. One evening—otherwise indistinguishable from the rest—I read aloud to them a story I had written only that afternoon, in a frenzy of creative freedom. And I remember Vomela on that occasion making a peculiar and pithy remark. *You'll do well for yourself* was all I think he said. And those heartfelt-sounding words meant a lot to me, seeing as I was about to make a life-altering decision, and coming from him, the true (if unrealized) artist, to me, who could only ever be an *approximator* of art, although by that time it was also quite clear that he thought himself a failure and that I with my naïveté and audacity had the makings of success, that his remark was therefore double-edged.

I remember arriving at Vomela's house on that winter's night expecting to be surprised, if not by the atmosphere then at least by his heady ingenuity, because of course I believed in him during the entire time I was away in America. My wish to see him in his artistic prime was almost granted when, after greeting those present, I took a look around his living space, which was now the empty swimming pool in his basement. This was a pool I still remembered crossing with breaststrokes during one of the fabulous birthday parties I attended here as a child. The more I considered my swimming across it, the more I thought this idea for a *swimming room* uncanny. I walked around the space and tried to grasp the sheer ingenuity of it. The pool's aquamarine walls were being gradually repainted, used as a surface for mixing colors. The artist's sketches and paintings were spread negligently over its blue tiled floor. One canvas may have been resting on an easel; I recall him actually working on a painting—on what was already an accomplished study of a woman's face—during the party, and as the night got older someone, some aspiring filmmaker in our midst, may have filmed the master at work. I realized instantly he sought here a creative isolation, his creativity compelling him to put that isolation on display inside a space that, true to its conception, would remain empty unless refilled with water. Technically, one could not shut the world out of a room that instead of a doorway had on either end a drop ladder, with neither ceiling nor canopy (but, to its credit, a bottom). What freedom, I thought as I lowered myself down into it. What perspective, I had to admit as soon as I set foot in it. But for these same reasons a sense of entrapment was unavoidable. The room was a form of aesthetic captivity. It was, strictly speaking, not a room but an *echo chamber*. And as soon as one sat on the sofa, the prospects to all sides began to shrink—a condition that no doubt affected the painter working here. To make one's home in such a space seemed almost a form of penance.

The following winter I spent among friends, meeting no one new. I saw Peter again on the second day of Christmas during midnight mass. We were both drinking in the park behind our parish church. I asked him about his art, which he insisted on calling his *hobby*, and so we got absolutely nowhere in what was to be our last conversation for some time. He did not let on he was drowning in his present circumstances; but his choice to move permanently into the basement—into such a basement, and even a notch below it—was to me a clear sign of alienation. Over the next two years I had no word of him, but one day my mother mentioned, by the by, that Vomela's *unlucky brother* had died of hypothermia somewhere in the Tatras. He apparently loved mountaineering; he had finally found a small passion he could fully explore.

POŻEGNANIE (1967-2000)

Nagła i tragiczna śmierć zabrała z naszego grona Michasia, człowieka niezwykłego. Był prawdziwym pasjonatem turystyki i rekreacji.

Potrafił w jeden dzień przejechać na rowerze Puszczę Kampinoską. Niestrudzenie przemierzał szlaki turystyczne różnych regionów Polski i zagranicy, dokumentując fotograficznie napotkane zabytki i pomniki przyrody. Szczególną uwagę poświęcił zabytkom sakralnym. Pozostała po Nim wspaniała kolekcja zdjęć kościołów wschodnich Niemiec z ostatniej wyprawy. Planował zwiedzić i opisać kościoły Rzymu.

Był nieprzeciętnie zdolny językowo, władał biegle niemieckim, holenderskim, angielskim, uczył się francuskiego. Jako ucznia i studenta cechował Go upór i wytrwałość w zdobywaniu wiedzy, ogromna ambicja i benedyktyńska pracowitość.

Osiągnięcia te były o tyle niezwykłe, bo dokonane przez człowieka, który w dzieciństwie uległ ciężkiemu wypadkowi. Nigdy nie odzyskał pełnej sprawności fizycznej. Trudno Mu było w naszym nietolerancyjnym społeczeństwie osiągnąć nie tylko sukces, ale choćby równorzędne traktowanie z ludźmi sprawnymi. Swoją pracowitością i uporem zdobył wykształcenie, zawód, realizował swoje hobby, był samodzielny.

Michaś był człowiekiem wprost ujmującego dobra, prawości, szczerości, przyjacielskiej lojalności i rodzinnej opiekuńczości. Do dziś widzę Go, jak w ulewnym deszczu jedzie na rowerze, by złożyć kwiaty na grobie ojca w dniu jego imienin. Nigdy nie odmówił pomocy, z czego był znany wśród sąsiadów. Kochał ludzi i zwierzęta, wzruszający był Jego stosunek do suki Lory, noszonej przez Niego na rękach po schodach, żeby nie bolały jej chore stawy.

Mimo trudnego życia i ogromu cierpień nie odwrócił się od Boga, był człowiekiem głęboko i niezwykle mądrze wierzącym; dawał świadectwo wiary nie tylko chodząc do kościoła, ale przede wszystkim w codziennej dobroci dla ludzi. Jego zapobiegliwość o rodzinę i dom wzruszała powszechnej szacunek – ileż pracy wkładał w prowadzenie bieżących domowych napraw czy pielęgnację ogrodu. Ze swojego okna zawsze podziwiałem z zachwytem efekty Jego ogrodniczej pasji.

Urzekające było Jego poczucie humoru, wolne od złośliwości wobec innych. Posiadał tę wielkość charakteru pozwalającą na autoironię w stosunku do własnej niezgrabności i niezręczności, ale nigdy nie szydził z ułomności czy wad bliźnich. Był pod tym względem bardzo tolerancyjny i wyrozumiały, czego nie zawsze sam doświadczał...

Nie ma już z nami Michasia i jest to trudne do zaakceptowania nie tylko dla Jego rodziny, ale też i dla mnie, Jego sąsiada i przyjaciela. Pocieszam się tylko, że jest teraz u boku swojego ukochanego ojca, który być może wyprosił u Boga, by oszczędził Michasiowi cierpień życia doczesnego i powołał Go tak wcześnie do Nieba.

Michasiu, chociaż nic Już nie będzie jak dawniej, a ul. Kossaka bez Ciebie jest pusta, to przecież Ty nadal żyjesz w naszej życzliwej pamięci i naszych ciepłych wspomnieniach. Ty już zaznajesz niebiańskiego spokoju, a my będziemy się modlić za Ciebie, aby nikt Ci w tym wypoczynku nie przeszkadzał.

WŁODZIMIERZ SZYSZKOWSKI

I went to see Vomela when I visited Poland that summer. Lora, his snarling Alsatian, was no longer around to escort strangers from the gate inside the house. His aging mother, of whom I caught a glimpse in the TV room, had shrunk from grief. The entire second storey was rented out to university students from Germany. He behaved as if nothing had happened. We talked briefly in the kitchen about the situation in Poland and parted on rather impersonal terms. I knew that he had meanwhile thrown himself into private enterprise, which I never suspected him of and to this day have not properly understood. Since that meeting, my contacts with those who could provide a coherent picture of his state of mind gradually petered out.

I could make less and less sense of the scattered facts I accumulated. I knew for instance that he had become withdrawn and, a "shadow of his former self," succumbed to narcotics and drink, but also that he was as gregarious as ever, that money turned his head, that, being generally upright and dependable, he went into cultural politics condemning the rampant opportunism that came with the territory, but was quickly growing bored, perhaps disillusioned. He made the news when he became director of the German-Polish Youth Organisation. He made the news again three years later with his resignation.

Was this, then, the slow death of a born artist? I will never know for certain. I am no longer privy to his life or even what became of him; for all I know, by now he may have made an all-defying recovery of his great talent. But I do know that he will never come into his own as an artist, never become the artist he was destined to be before life got in the way. It was clear he had been thwarted by his own indomitable standards, and by his unwillingness (or inability) to seek legitimation anywhere but in a state institution. It was not enough for him that we, his peers, endorsed him; for that he was too traditional in his thinking and too prudently initiated into art. He wanted to be an innovator in the tradition of the Old Masters—not, therefore, at any cost. And this was his mistake, as well as proof of his time-bound genius; both meant he would never win out in modern painting.

But it is also not entirely true that Peter and I "went our separate ways." On my side, the earlier bonds of friendship and habit have been replaced not by estrangement but by affinity, which grew substantially with our distance. Though I have pursued my art *illegitimately* for many years, I am oppressed by a sense of futility. I wanted desperately to escape my middle-class material situation for a situation of intellectual patronage much like his own, hoping artistic credibility would be among the payoffs. I did manage to get out of the former, then find something to the effect of the latter, though I have nothing to show for it.

Generally speaking, I am a calculating person—but know that terrific things can arise out of miscalculations. The need to write about my friend Peter, for example, went against all my expectations. I merely sat down with the intention to finish reading a book, one I had been dying to finish and, as I had indeed calculated, could have finished that same afternoon, but for taking up the pen. Suddenly I felt an urge to reminisce about the *poolroom*, wanted to steep myself in this reminiscence, but as soon as I began thinking about it I was keen on writing about it. There followed what can be described alternately as an "avalanche of ideas," a "thunderstorm of images," or a "torrent of words," many of which were exaggerated, most of which were true.

F. W.

(09.23.07)

They are predicting record levels of snowfall this winter, and record levels of rainfall next summer.

To me, your presence is a distant memory. Week after week, we stare in one direction, but the object we fasten upon each time grows more remote. We search our memory like a receding shoreline and discern only the contours of approaching absence. How is it that your expressions are no clearer in my mind for having lost their dynamism? In well-lit conditions, from a reasonable distance, the stasis of an object gives it clarity and distinctness—such that we say it has *etched itself on our mind.* But the visibility was poor where I had seen you, and the light conditions of memory deteriorate over time, blurring even the starkest outlines and dulling the most vibrant colors.

I spent the larger part of this year working on a study of nostalgia. Two days ago I passed some hours in the library tying up the loose ends of my research. On my way out, I took a detour through the audiovisual section to retrieve a film I had been meaning to see again. You make your way through the dusky hall towards the counter. Awaiting your turn, you survey the partitioned interior, the aura of television screens now in use. You are assigned a screening booth, which drastically narrows your field of view. The soundproofing seals off your auditory canals until you plug in the headset handed to you and turn on one of the media players. You await sound; sound is the cue to direct your sight to the monitor and screen out the remainder of your environment.

But Brakhage preferred silence: most of his films demand it. A silent "by Brakhage" film is more than a silent picture. Sound stuffed with silence, like ears with cotton wool, and relegated to memory. I start the disc and am instantly engrossed in the filmmaker's diverse nostalgias: nature nostalgia, cosmic nostalgia, womb nostalgia . . . Affective states and perceptions are frequently rendered not in real-time but as daydream-memories, patterned after acts of recollection. The result is then a microscopy of nostalgia.

Here are films as if exposed beneath closed eyelids. Brakhage is said to document subjectivity to the extent this is possible (imaginable). In *The Stars Are Beautiful* he drops this curious statement: "Retention colors are the only true colors." Brakhage the magician of light patterns on the retina—and their afterimages. The flashes that sometimes make for intervals between scenes signal some mystery, which is their lining, or which coats them. Their abruptness secures their obscurity and calls for a hermeticism of vision bound up with memory, as it is in sentient organisms. The "wold" of *The Wold Shadow* is a tenebrous tapestry of trees flooded by light (natural? artificial?) of variable temperature, coherence, intensity. Or a nighttime forest discharging itself in bursts of radiant energy. Or a camera-eye blinking with variable aperture and speed, the brightness and color values of the wold (the subject) first positive, then not, then blurred, then clouded by frozen cataracts of paint. The *wold shadow* is there: memory of shadows cast by each of these three possibilities. Enchanted, dizzy with excitement, I leave the library blinking to revive what I had just seen and project it onto the early evening.

Retention color: is it an aftervision, excited in the eye by incandescence or luminescence? The colored trace of some bright appearance? Diametrical opposite and spectral complement of a color removed from view? Such evanescent impressions, retained further by blinking, were once seen as morbid. They indicated a susceptibility of the organ of sight and its "inability to recover itself." "[N]ot to be wondered at in the case of dazzling lights," wrote the venerable Goethe. "If any one looks at the sun, he may retain the image in his eyes for several days," in rare cases even several years (*Theory of Colors*).

Retention color: is it not a *Gedächtnisfarbe*, or memory-color: the stable color attributed to a material object, based on the dominant color memory of its previous viewings, standing for the real color of that object (the *constant* color beyond the inconstancy of its perceived coloring)? Or is it something more evanescent, a recognition color normally withheld from view?

Retention color: the name suggests that it retains or is retained, instead of fading with the rest of them. But this persistence of vision by way of slow decay—it too is subject to fading, and its fading must be all the more remarkable for being late in coming. Is it not simply the fading memory or specter of a color once perceived? For the enlightened Locke (who would not let himself be dazzled by reason) memories are painted in the mind with such fading colors; their retention rested on their restoration through recollection.

And in this sense it is that our ideas are said to be in our memories, when indeed they are actually nowhere, but only there is an ability in the mind when it will to revive them again, and as it were paint them anew on itself, though some with more, some with less difficulty; some more gaily, and others more obscurely. And thus it is, by the assistance of this faculty, that we are said to have all those ideas in our understandings which, though we do not actually contemplate, yet we can bring in sight, and make appear again, and be the objects of our thoughts, without the help of those sensible qualities which first imprinted them there. But yet there seems to be a constant decay of all our ideas, even of those which are struck deepest, and in minds the most retentive; so that if they be not sometimes renewed, by repeated exercise of the senses, or reflection on those kinds of objects which at first occasioned them, the print wears out, and at last there remains nothing to be seen. Thus the ideas, as well as children, of our youth, often die before us: and our minds represent to us those tombs to which we are approaching; where, though the brass and marble remain, yet the inscriptions are effaced by time, and the imagery moulders away. The pictures drawn in our minds are laid in fading colours; and if not sometimes refreshed, vanish and disappear.

When I confront my personal memories with reality, with facts sharply defined, with the vivid reminiscences of others, I realize my negligence. Whole tracts of time were lived and one thought no more of them; whole ages have fallen into desuetude. Looking for them now is like chasing dust around an empty house. But on this occasion—occasioned by this writing effort, which as you now see has also become an effort of memory—I sit down to retouch my faded icons. The operation demands loud colors, the loudest possible, yet these too are marred by oblivion. Memory is not a treasure trove that, laid open, dazzles us with its contents. It is a shadowy pit.

F. W.

(10.01.07)

Leaving aside the absurdity of the effort—to debunk Newton's *Opticks* (1704), his color doctrine, by that time a scientific truism—Goethe's *Theory of Colors* (1810) was rife with insight into the experience of color and, as he had hoped, of value to artists. Take, for instance, his explanation of *chiaroscuro*. Several *forms* are invoked to make this phenomenon intelligible to any manner of reader. The simplest form is the cube: "the three sides of which that are seen represent the light, the middle the tint, and the shadow in distinct order." Next in complexity: an open book (this gives Goethe away). Then, the polygon, exhibiting "artist-like treatment in which all kinds of lights, half-lights, shadows, and reflexions, would be appreciable." Of natural objects, a cluster of grapes is said to exemplify "a picturesque completeness in chiaro-scuro." Indeed, *spheres* are "perfect example[s] of natural chiaro-scuro" (exceptions: Sun, stars).

If there is any natural phenomenon I detest, it is precisely the sun—the whole *heliotropic sphere* of life. I prefer to sit and think, prefer to rest, in the umbrage of the tall cypress out back or in my sunless front room, the light mostly kept out by blinds. This is a general preference, as my eyes are normally light-sensitive. After the operation I am (quite sensibly) light-phobic and my four walls are gloom itself. But since my eyes were slit, opened, and repaired I can see far better—though, honestly, I didn't expect to see any better, having been a wearer of corrective lenses my entire life. In light of the marked improvement, on the day following the surgery I disposed of the everyday optical devices I kept around the house, all useless now—everything except my prism, really more of a bauble. "Color itself is a degree of darkness" (already back to reading Goethe!), it is "allied to shadow, so it combines readily with it."[1] If doubt is shadow, a state of mind rife with colors, then certainty is plain white light. Prisms disperse certainty. I put mine on the bedside.

A jolt of pain is fine once in a while, but who likes illness? Personally, there is nothing I dread more than bouts of physical suffering. I suffer embarrassment when having to admit infirmity of any kind, let alone the kind that bars me from activity. I am always humiliated by my sickness; I am already half in the spirit world, am I not? Already half buried, am I not? But even when sick, one must continue one's creative, one's intellectual labors. One must *work with* an illness to *work through* the illness. One must recognize it as an opportunity (rather than a negation of opportunity) and take advantage of it—an effort, first, of recognition, second, of application, is needed to make the most of being unwell. We must reframe the pathology as a unique set of physical and mental parameters, placing us in an altered social state, putting at our disposal a different set of perspectives and concerns, which can be not only useful in our work but actually help us work through the disease. We must be prepared to lay hold of these hidden benefits to work our way *out of* the illness ravaging us—which, incidentally, must never be taken for our unconscious revolt against our work, but ascribed instead to extraneous circumstances, to be met in turn with our opposition. We must reap our intellectual strength from the most affected parts, the most inflamed loci of an illness. If, for instance, we are racked with fever, incapacitating and even life-threatening, we must will ourselves to run a *creative* fever, just as high, delirious and *death-threatening.* Any work can be accomplished while bedbound—for me it is studying

---

[1] Who stops to ponder the ageless standoff between sun and color? In your southern parts, where both are at their most intense—the sun the fiercest antagonist of color, color the most defiant towards the sun—a northern temperament cannot but wonder at the powers of the burning sun and the potencies of color. In places, rapprochements seem possible (ceramics); elsewhere color seems vanquished for good (wooden shutters); still elsewhere it renews itself with stunning regularity (clothes). Ultimately, I do not know which is greater to behold: the fading of color, or its provocation by the sun? An outsider can only watch that "corrida" from the shade.

and writing—and any work can become our cure given the right dosage. And there is nobody more qualified than us to prescribe the curative amount. We ought to work wildly when sick, especially when sick, even if we are made sicker by it, so that we turn our work into auto-homeopathy. If we are committed to our work, we are as good as married to it; we stand by it symptomatic and asymptomatic, in sickness and in health, 'til death finally do us part.

I feel fully myself through pain, drawing from it the full sensation of existence, a simple affirmation of being. That is the *real* source of my hypochondria—in sickness I find an imperative to continue my work, its completion becomes that much more urgent. As I am recuperating, I consider: what riles me and gets me so febrile is that my work (my writing), if finished (rather than aborted), would be *sampled* (rather than read through), yet only in this latter method of reading, like eating hors d'oeuvres, would my *creative process* be reconstituted. You make a work whole only so others can take away with them its fragments. You can strive all you want for lucidity of reflection/expression but others will only ever see it darkly, that is to say misunderstand almost everything you write or, for that matter, do. But in my already delirious state this twofold frustration (which would have stymied me instantly had I been well) is thoroughly invigorating. I relish the absurd challenges of work pursued in a sickbed. What can be more exhilarating than actually *completing* the work in such a state, and with this completion defeating the illness? It is much the same if an ailment brings about enervation, a weakening of one's constitution. Carrying on one's work depends then on decelerating cognition to an uncomfortable rate, to an almost *painful* slowness compared even with drug-drowsed thought. Extraordinary ideas spring as much from racing as from *plodding* mental activity; what serves creativity the least are mental moderation and the functional *concord* between mind and body. Ill thought should always be at least two leagues behind or ahead of the (enervated or high-strung) body. Slowly letting out the wick or burning up like a firework. You feel your mind is going, your sanity is taking leave of you, but such thoughts should be spliced with the slow-burning wick or a coruscating sparkler rod. Your mind may just as well be taking you along, and you just as well taking your leave of sanity. Disease can darken your wits like that and make you *tone-deaf:* you can't hum along to your most progressive or most regressive thoughts, the only ones worth carrying a tune for. You come down with something nasty, but the best thing you can do, instead of letting the illness have its way with you and take its natural course in you, instead of calling in a doctor, is to overcome the highly debilitating sense of your *mental abnormality*—such a sense being the norm when one has really gotten sick, since if the body is acting up, so we reason, the mind is acting up with it (Descartes would be ashamed of us), this self-consciousness arising of course from our fear of and capitulation to disease, to an abnormal physiological condition, however common it may be around us. We would rather abstain from touching our work in such a state for fear of corrupting it with a tainted mind (a mind in need of quarantine!). But about the best thing we can do for ourselves and our work is become an instrument of our disease; the way to do it is, actually, by exercising volition—not by giving up and harmonizing mentally with our bodies, but by sowing *discord* between mind and body. The commonality of ill health, all the wide-spread physical suffering, makes one prone to sympathetic vibration with other strained bodies—*but this is not yet music!*

Consider Schopenhauer's analogy: the relations between our will (desire), obstacles to the will's (desire's) realization, our knowledge of these obstacles (memory, consciousness), and pain (spiritual or physical) he compares to the relations between parts of a musical instrument. "[T]he will is the string, its frustration or impediment the vibration of the string, knowledge the sounding-board, and pain the sound" ["On the Suffering of the World"]. Compare Monsieur Teste's logbook entry: "Pain is musical, we can almost speak of it in musical terms. There are sharps and flats, andantes and furiosos,

sustained notes, rests, arpeggios, progressions—sudden silences, etc."
Now, after this pessimist *Stimmung* (Schopenhauer's) and cerebral
libretto (Valéry's), consider the actual movement of afflicted thought:
"Each illness is a musical problem—the healing a musical solution
[but also dissolution, *Auflösung*]. The shorter and more complete
the solution [dissolution], the greater the musical talent of the physician. Sickness demands manifold solutions. The selection of the
most appropriate solution determines the talent of the physician."
And, just two entries down (still Novalis): "The physician's art is
indeed the art of slaying." The medical virtuoso hears us off, hearing
out the sound's decay into silence. The ambiguity of *Auflösung*—
solution and dissolution—has been resolved; the ultimate, the most
effective cure is death. Novalis, claimed by consumption at a young
age, recorded these ailing movements in his aphoristic *Enzyklopädie*,
working the pen like a tuning fork.

The color scale corresponded to the musical scale (so Newton).

It is already getting on to noon. Street sounds outside ampli-
fied over the white trickling sound of electricity inside. You part the
blinds and peer out, but not so fast: the eyes must first adjust to light
for objects to adopt shapes and colors. Sickness and life are really
equally obscure. The outside no clearer that the inside, perceptions
no clearer than memories.

F. Wren

(10.09.07)

I continue.

After more than two months' absence I return to the library for books. The trip, made with a vacant mind (and the references I needed written out), proves a catalyst for half-forgotten memories of a dream. They come unannounced and, as I sit down to write this note, already have to actively be recalled, pulled out of memory as from a swamp.

Last night, while a storm was brewing and while it erupted, I dreamt a dream in three parts, or three dreams that belonged together. I remember that as soon as I stirred from sleep, I began dreaming the next—its ally, its adversary? I do not see any distinctive kinship or conflict before recounting them; instead, I am struck by a more or less subtle progression of signification. They seem to be gesturing in one direction.

The first dream: two women. Related, sisters perhaps, the shorter, stouter one self-effacing, the taller and elder of a frank disposition. Their manner of dress circa 1930. The dream obviously spun from impressions of a photograph reproduced in the previous day's paper, of *Anne and Margot Frank on the Zandvoort Seashore.* The girls stand dressed in identical patterned summer clothing, their backs turned to the camera, Margot then a head above her sister.

The pair in my dream were much older and also wore identical out-
fits (women's skirt-suits of a uniform color). There were some other
parallels besides. I am charged with showing these two around a city
I cannot recognize: too European for America, and still too American for Europe. One of our stops is a Holocaust memorial. Its design
is minimalist, petrifying in its rough, stony obstinacy. Across the
long hollowed-out rock, vaguely suggestive of a gas chamber, a grate
or fence is installed, the cavity behind it filled with solid metal. In
this molten mass human silhouettes can only barely be discerned,
suggesting a throng of people. The forward incline of this *human
mass* gives the impression of scarcely contained panic. The women I

am accompanying confess their ignorance: they know nothing of the *Totenlager*, had never heard of them. Their memory ends in 1939 (like breaking off in mid-sentence, I say to myself), presumably the year of their death. They tell me they are here to admire the wonders of the modern age. Still faintly incredulous, they are saddened to learn things had gone so awry. We leave the monument in silence, along feuillemort sidewalks (it is autumn and leaves lie thick on the ground), until we come to what I describe to them as a modern place of worship. We enter a church of sorts. The interior is spacious and plain, full of natural light flowing from a skylit dome. Every inch of wall is of exposed uniform brickwork. There are quite a few people inside. The congregation, if one may call it that, is organized around a variety of social services and activities. Next to the seltzer fountain someone distributes lebkuchen, another puts out bins with second-hand clothing, a third picks up litter. At first my two women seem to take little note of this bustle, alarmed as they are by the absence of an altar. I point out a massive analogue clock on the front wall, where one would normally find the pipe organ. This tempers their dismay somewhat. Very soon, resigned to the change of customs, they sit down at one of the aisle tables and unwrap their sandwiches. They appear content with the communal-recreational purpose of the place, the *Gemeindetempel* as they refer to it in private, and smile at the children flicking bottle caps at their feet.

The second dream: a cemetery. I pull into a prestigious Jewish cemetery to visit my grave. It is an open secret that as a child I went missing and was taken for dead. Because my body could not be found, a gold locket was buried in my place. Now, years later, I return (alive) to reclaim the locket as my inheritance. Visitors to the cemetery are required to sign the register and leave their coat and bags in the vestibule. My grave stands just off the main path and I am led there by one of the gloved ushers. I remove the lid and reach inside, but the urn contains only a lock of hair, a torn film strip, and a sheet of paper with illegible scrawl. Distressed at this discovery, I complain to the superintendent, describe the missing—the *stolen!*— necklace, and demand he recover it. I do not know the outcome of the ensuing search, only that it involved Interpol and figures in uniform. I believe the dream continued, although I could not extend my recollection beyond this point.

The third dream: a play. I am the author of this play and agree to act in it. Unlike the others, I am not a professional actor. Our stage is a small gymnasium with rugged floorboards. The spectators sit in the adjoining storeroom on narrowly graduated benches and view the show through a small doorway. Among them I recognize two poet-playwrights: one a former flame, a Finn, the other a former student, a Jew. We go ahead with the play without my having rehearsed even once. The performance consists of unsynchronized movement across the room in random clusters and of the odd word hurled into the air by this or that actor. This barebones spectacle evidently does not appeal to the audience. Afterwards, we wait for applause squeezed inside a wardrobe the size of a pantry, as the theatre director strains to catch any reaction whatsoever, though it is clear there is none forthcoming. My play is almost universally panned. Only in reviews written by my Finn and the Jew does it receive equal praise.

I knew immediately after recording them what the three dreams *indicated*, but not how or why. Why three such dreams, why such oneiric persistence without any apparent trigger in my waking life? And what was their significance for the dreamer? A dream-reference, that is to say a *repressive* reference, is no direct way of addressing a matter, but—rather more problematically—a totally indirect, involuntary way of doing so. It occurred to me that in the act of writing the full meaning of one's words also remains, to a degree, *repressed*, and that actual progress in one's written work often depends on lifting or breaking through the repression, whereby one gains access to the latent content of the work, which is to say to its deeper significance. This in turn offers incentives to mine the work of the unconscious (for what is easier than unconscious work?), provided one has the mental stamina for it (for what is more difficult than digging in the unconscious?). The purpose of these my reflections was, at any rate, to claim the dream-work that gave rise to the three of dreams as a legitimate part of the work at hand—though hardly *in hand!*

Of course, relaying the dreams and subjecting them to analysis which yielded evidence of *Shoah-logic*—a subliminal preoccupation with the tragedy of European Jews—could be dismissed as trite or tendentious. As I saw it, only by recounting the dreams would their significance, their individual and cumulative significance, be brought to light. Yet this significance continued to elude me. It was not until weeks later, after coming across a line by Blanchot—my habitual line of reasoning all but dispersed by *The Writing of the Disaster*— that their overarching import became thinkable, as did the import of each one. At this point, with everything committed to paper and succeeded by nightmares, I had already lost the detailed memory of the dreams (I might not have even been able to recall their order). Consequently, I could not bend them to that *revealed* meaning by leaving out or exaggerating at will certain elements of my account; it would have been unconvincing. I had only the original record to go on, hastily jotted down the next morning and overwriting my fading recollection. What struck me upon reading the notes again was that this initial recording, which I resolved never to tamper with so as to leave open the possibility of unearthing the true significance in the future, was that each dream could be construed as a reference to the Shoah without any pieces of the dream-puzzle left unused. In other words, once I alighted on and accepted such a reading, everything about the dreams appeared to support it. Not only did each dream invite such an interpretation, but the entire dream-suite manifested the inexorable logic of the Shoah. What is more—and this seemed only added proof of its validity—I was thoroughly uneasy about the interpretation (as the above passages make clear).

The dreams' meanings can be summarized as follows. The first reflected the obliviousness of the German *Volk* to the fate of German

Jewry in the Third Reich. Both ethnic groups appear conflated in the two women (siblings?), who are, on the one hand, modeled on the Frank sisters and, on the other, find enjoyment in the relaxed atmosphere of the "temple," highly evocative for me of a neo-pagan gathering. The second dream stood for vehement anti-Semitism (the stereotype of the Jew as devious and gold-obsessed) and its consequences (the theft of valuables, the symbolic burial of hair and photographic documentation where remains where unavailable). The third, in relation to the other two and as the last one in the sequence, showed that fraternity between Jew and gentile was possible in those difficult times (very few Jews were deported from Finland)—a fraternity within the world of art, all its bellicosity and spuriousness notwithstanding. If these interpretations seem overstated, it is because through dreaming and writing the three dreams have become threaded together in my mind.

F. Wren

(10.15.07)

We are presently wavering in the greatest blackout, one of the interior as well as, above all, of the exterior and the superior, that has ever occurred in history.

Ernst Bloch, *The Spirit of Utopia*

Night; white, sleepless night—such is the disaster: the night lacking darkness, but brightened by no light.

The calm, the burn of the holocaust, the annihilation of noon—the calm of the disaster.

Maurice Blanchot, *The Writing of the Disaster*

Rolety zaciemniające, ul. Nowolipki 18
[Blackout blinds, 18 Nowolipki Street]

sign in confectioner's window, Warsaw, 1942

Since uncovering the hidden significance of those dreams, I have not stopped thinking about the *personal and moral* significance of the Shoah. Learning about it has fired up my imagination time and again, but what have I drawn from this besides a stunted aesthetic loathing of Nazi machinery, efficacy, iconography, ritual? I owe my hateful appreciation of Nazism to the lens of Riefenstahl and innumerable documentaries, to Kracauer's critiques and Sebald's oblique narratives, to repeated visits to Treblinka and Auschwitz-Birkenau, but, most importantly, to growing up in a country once primed for destruction at the hands of Hitler's men. In effect, I have cultivated a detached knowledge of the Holocaust; the Holocaust as abstraction, as mechanism, as mathematical object always seemed more alluring to me than the concrete historical reality. In effect, I have been more concerned with the impossibility of witnessing and with evil's profound banality than with any moral lessons for my own life. Perhaps

I feared the visceral contemplation of sadism and murder as morally degrading. Perhaps I inherited the collective mortification at having allowed it to happen. Most likely, beneath these excuses lay a valid reason: my early consciousness of the futility of trying to confront the catastrophe through image, speech, or writing. Without having witnessed it, all one could hope for was acute awareness of this past and reassurances of its pastness. Not a comprehensive understanding, even if one could gather and itemize every directive, procedure, and victim. Only a vague sense of the event. Perhaps an understanding of the causal links between all the microevents, but not a feeling of having understood the macroevent, equivalent to lack of understanding. But the dreams broke the ice of my skepticism and my insouciance. All of a sudden I knew that the language of dreams was in so many ways ideal for conceiving of the Shoah and living with its consequences: a dissembling language disinterested in the disaster it alluded to (again alluding to Blanchot).

My aesthetic distance from the Nazi crimes told me that all the years of my American Holocaust-education have not shaken my moral security. I had no doubt about my own imperviousness to extremes and corruption. No doubt about my *incapacity* ever to take part in a plot leading to murder or mass murder, or any reprehensible act on racial, religious, and other grounds. I saw no need to prepare for the eventuality of being faced with gross moral choices (of the kind made by the Nazi killers after the solution, the system, the apparatus, the numbers were disclosed to them). All the while I was reasoning along these lines, I've come to realize I was busy skirting the pedagogical question (what did I "get" from it all?). But, as you know, the byways of consciousness verge on madness. We assume ourselves incapable of atrocity; it was (we reason) the doing of a monstrous madman (genius) who despite deluded supremacy and the pride he must have felt in masterminding and conducting a symphony of death, of orchestrating and overseeing the disaster, was ready to cast himself at any point into the pandemonium he thought he commanded, as the most impure of all, most scorned of all, most elevated in his scorn—who had fundamentally no regard for life, for real, workaday existence, and who led his hungry wolf-pack into a *silva obscura*. But Hitler was just the tip of the iceberg (we reason), in which the other perpetrators were voluntarily or involuntarily entrapped. Here we break down: what an inhuman disaster, unnatural, inhuman catastrophe, what animals, *animals*—and what a soothing mantra it is. But the disaster's actual return remains inconceivable to us. The monsters have fallen under the rubble. So our guard is not held high enough. We would rather not look past the horizon of history, nor dig through the piles (and pits) of historical debris, sorted and unsorted documents, partial and impartial memories; we would rather not move beyond these *obstructions*.

There is today so much nostalgia (we observe) for destruction on the grandest scale. Hitlerism continues to evoke in us a morbid curiosity, exert on us its magnetic pull. This despite all the teaching and learning about the Holocaust that has been going on for over sixty years, so that one is tempted to conclude that all this indoctrination has been of no use, has done little to dampen and more to foment our fascination with incarnate evil. No talk about the Holocaust—be it formal or informal—is ever free of didacticism. I have never been *unattended* on a trip to Auschwitz—educators or family were always around to remind me about the moral significance of every square foot of that museum. A passing mention of the Holocaust is always already a *lesson* about the Holocaust, *in nuce* a history and philosophy lesson. *With the implementation of the Final Solution, human reason showed its true colors . . .* The didacticism of my earliest Holocaust-education made me balk at such learning. What does it even mean to learn from the Holocaust? *How* can one learn from it? The evidence is overabundant ("the most documented event in history"), but the event falls apart in one's head. You don't deny it, yet incomprehension invites you to think like it never really happened. But the three dreams revealed my subliminal compunction about freewheeling in this way. One absolutely must (I now see) think the unthinkable, imagine its most unimaginable details, and prepare oneself for the eventuality of being capable of or being manipulated into evil and, in effect, of participating in destruction of horrific proportions. One must study Hitler and the Holocaust like one studies the palm of one's hand—not out of antiquarian but of *chiromantic* interest.

I have asked other people the same pedagogical question. Since it was not one they could simply shrug off, they had to acknowledge that they have no answer, or that their answer would consist of platitudes they would rather not utter, or that roundabout answers were overlong and required too much of them. Those whom I managed to engage in some rudimentary reflection on the subject, feeling themselves encouraged by the fact that I myself had no satisfactory words, exhibited a similar *sliding of moral responsibility under aestheticism* (such as I myself felt guilty of). They were easily distracted from contemplating the crime as such by the clichés, the context, the desideratum, and the logistics of the crime, by the great ironies of rationality, which at its extreme admits barbarity, by the industrialization of death and the perverse charisma of the criminals, so that repeatedly I had to bring into focus for them the crime itself. The Holocaust is a litmus test for modern morality. We have found our moral litmus test in an inscrutable, insoluble, diabolically elaborate historical event. If you are against it, you are fundamentally good, if you are for it, or deny it existed, you are fundamentally ill, evil, or both. Even if you test positive, you cross-examine yourself on the degree of your positivity: am I compassionate enough—are there limits to my tolerance—am I really free of prejudice?

If one is drawn to violence and death (the result of violence, of one's justice and another's injustice) one cannot help turning into a pessimist. If one is attracted to lost causes and futile resistance, one is the vehicle of an ardent pessimism. The ardent pessimist is happier than the ordinary pessimist, who gives up on a life of contentment and exerts himself only as far as justifying his stance; happier, too, than the misanthrope. I once thought I would end up a misanthrope, but I did not. Once a misanthrope, always a misanthrope; there is nothing one can do about it, ressentiment and self-loathing are mixed up in the vitriol reserved for humanity as a whole. But the pessimist is like a man standing on the Moon and casting his eyes back at Earth: full of pity for this brittle ship of fools sailing through a black universe. Within the span of three decades the best possible world (Leibniz) became the worst possible world (Schopenhauer). Every potential do-gooder became at heart an evildoer. We live in this world and our hearts pump the blood of evildoers. By Schopenhauer's lights, we live in a world where evil is the positive value, suffering the only concrete experience, and goodness and pleasure ephemeral and negative:

> As a reliable compass for orienting yourself in life, and banishing all doubt as to the right way of looking at it, nothing is more useful than to accustom yourself to regarding this world as a place of atonement, a penitentiary, a sort of a *penal colony* . . . This outlook will enable us to view the so-called imperfections of the majority of men, i.e. their moral and intellectual deficiencies and the facial appearance resulting therefrom, without surprise and certainly without indignation . . . The conviction that the world, and therefore man too, is something which really ought not to exist is in fact calculated to instil in us indulgence towards one another: for what can be expected of beings placed in such a situation as we are?

We are obliged to look grimly at the world, to regard the world in its hopeless decrepitude, and not try to lift the world out of its decrepitude, which would only sink it deeper into hopelessness. The Holocaust is the zenith of history, the defeat of Nazism its nadir.

Holocaust—zenith of history.

F. Wren

63

(10.24.07)

A brute fact: even great books are bought and sold by the pound. And the scale does not measure their artistic-intellectual weight, only their physical weight. The tragedy of *being an object* and turning one's thought into *an object of public perusal* is that there exists no objective measure of content, only of form—that form as the more reliable measure receives greater priority over subjective measurements, as measurements of content are liable to be.

The solitude of art-objects can be compared only to our solicitude towards them. Once out, a work of art cannot be taken in; it necessarily, *by definition*, overruns the confines of mind and space. But nothing is as fragile and therefore as vulnerable as an artwork; the fragility so typical of it is all its own. Once out, a work never fully escapes abuse because it never fully escapes attention. One could safely say that the more attention a work receives, the more victimized it is and the more it suffers—critically, but also physically. Some artists accept the maltreatment of art as an essential part of the appreciation of art. Some even provoke it with controversies and scandalous innovation. Some try to work around or prevent abuse of their works by manhandling them themselves, by making their works (or their parts) replaceable, or by executing them in some durable material. But the latter comes at a price; a durable piece of art is naturally less artistic; its beauty, sublimity and ingenuity combined do not move us as strongly as fragile beauty, which moves us to pity for the impermanence of all things. In this light, the natural decay of artwork is itself artistic.

Whatever its value, every work of art without exception remains mute, unable to represent, much less defend, itself against charges of profanity or its own profanation. Always at the mercy of history and art historians—but always first at the mercy of the artist. No-one conjured the physical vicissitudes of artwork as perspicuously as Heidegger in an essay written on the edge of the Black Forest and World War Two:

The picture hangs on the wall like a rifle or a hat. A painting, e.g., the one by Van Gogh that represents a pair of peasant shoes, travels from one exhibition to another. Works of art are shipped like coal from the Ruhr and logs from the Black Forest. During the First World War Hölderlin's hymns were packed in the soldier's knapsack together with cleaning gear. Beethoven's quartets lie in the storerooms of the publishing house like potatoes in a cellar. ["Origin of the Work of Art"]

Consider the case of written work. If *as a mental event* it is singular and hopelessly original, then *as an object* it is duplicable and hopelessly unoriginal: always only a stack of papers. Whether the artist's original or the printer's copy, always only some spilled ink. It may well be an event—the writing or reading of a book, often called a reading- or writing-experience—but it is also, at the same time and *quite hopelessly*, an object: the page covered with text, the book in front of you. Written work (like painted work) is always at once fluid and solid: in the act of writing its fluidity becomes replaced by solidity, and in the act of reading, this solidity by another fluidity. The experience of being surprised by a book you had in fact already read (and thoroughly enjoyed), not recognizing a thing about this book, but being merely confronted with its thingness—that experience is all too familiar. It is the experience of the gap between artistic work and the work of art.

This thingness of books, especially of many books kept in a small space, stacked high without rhyme or reason, can become oppressive. I worry about being oppressed by the books I own—quite different from being oppressed by the ownership of books. There are days when I am certainly very oppressed by the presence of so many books in such a small space. There is really no more room for me with them around, just as there is no room for more books with me around. Yet I keep introducing new books, and reintroducing books that had either fallen or been misplaced and have now been picked up or found, or those I had lent (both with relief at the extra space and with apprehension at never seeing them again) and that have just been returned to me. So now: loads and loads of books everywhere, and the fear that they will all come falling down one moment as I am passing through (or edging through) or sitting or (worse) dozing in my armchair, and that I or (more so) that they might be injured in the fall. The idea of all those books tipping over or (even) a shelf detaching itself from the wall and crashing to the floor, is positively nerve-wracking. Every time a book is taken off a shelf, transposed or put back I feel I am pushing my luck. I have so far been unusually lucky in avoiding an avalanche of book matter. I do believe a little order goes a long way, and that the ordering of books and maintaining always some semblance of order are possibly the best way of obviating the clutter typical of book-laden apartments. One really cannot speak of a book collection without having taken stock and organized and subjected one's books to a more or less logical and consistent access-and-retrieval system. In apartments where the number of books impedes one's access to them and exceeds a sustainable human-to-book ratio, books attract a frightful degree of clutter in a category unto itself. If it were merely dust and cobwebs everything would still be manageable; but a book heaven that has not been whipped into shape invites its owner to *let go* of themselves, is an invitation to physical sloth, if not intellectual sloth and downright mental confusion (too many books in too much chaos too often proves deadly for a thinking brain). The typical flat where books predominate, hence a space dominated by books, sooner or later adapts to the physical dimensions of books and reconfigures itself to accommodate even more of them—that is, ceases to be a flat and becomes a library. The sole occupant of such a space is, properly speaking, sharing accommodation. Without realizing it, this inhabitant has already given up many of the advantages of living alone. For starters, there is the uncontrollable, self-begetting clutter. You can deceive yourself that you could straighten up any day, but the mess that comes with a preponderance of books is addictive and ineradicable. It takes considerable exertion of the will to alter this reality. Similarly, you may claim to be free to move out any day, to leave the mess and cramped conditions behind, but the truth is only too material: you are not going anywhere as long as you hold on to this many books. There is, finally, the sheer lack of space for independent thought. These towers of intellect are known for their diminishing effects. You feel dwarfed both physically and mentally, and when this inequality in stature becomes too great you are done for as an independent thinker. Intellectual inferiority won't let you scale the shoulders of giants to see further than them.

On less lucid evenings, every library is a haunted cemetery. You have heard that a work is stillborn as a book, physically smothered between two covers, wrapped in the title and end pages, buried on a shelf: a little corpse of a book haunted by the little ghost of writing. Of course, every page of every book is consecrated, should be put away with important papers—never scrapped, used to wrap fish or start stove fires. A living space that has acquired the smell, look and layout of a library, that is to say, no longer contains a private library but has instead become a library in a private home (ordinarily through the conscious effort of its owner to furnish it with books), is as it were on sacred burial ground. It is particularly unsettling to become aware of this when alone with your private excess (god knows, nobody around has crammed so much into such a space) and the clutter that has become its status quo (no point in tidying up or even airing the place), although just a moment ago you may have felt fortunate in the intimacy of so many great books and minds. But the spookiest thought is always that of being buried alive by your books, crushed by their weight as by a crumbling edifice, without knowing what precipitated their collapse. This is a nightmare I may have had more than once. The library, so crucial for a writer, shows me its sinister side.

Consider books again. The materiality of a published book is indistinguishable from the materiality of millions of other volumes, and the virtual reproduction of the book is just that—mimicry of its characterless ("iconic") physical appearance. It is only fair to say of such a book: an object to be picked up, turned over, put down again.

When one is writing a book, one is torn between three impulses: to produce something worthy of a book, have it published, distributed and sold; to deny everything one has already produced; and also to hide one's work as soon as it is finished to protect it from objectification as *a book*. You sweat over it, you pour your blood into it, but as a book a work is finished, dead, open to decomposition.

Even so, a pound of book is not a pound of flesh. The most extravagant period in the history of the book—when it was inscribed onto parchment and bound in hide—is long over. Modern books are organically dissociated from bodies. Continuity between book and flesh is a *lost art*. No-one writes books with blood anymore (this may yet change with Partington's Blood Pen!). It is in the book's constitution to resemble its maker (an open book = an open mind, a closed book = an enigma) but contiguity between man and book occurs less and less. This "rewiring" is a mistake; contact between man and book is psychologically illuminative. Like men, books do not come by character with age but through more or less vulgar interactions. They should be tattered, spat upon, mutilated, singed, etc . . . I own four books whose physicality holds value for me, books with character, books with which I sometimes imagine myself interconnected. And I shall describe them here, noting down their distinctive characteristics.

Title: *The Hound of the Baskervilles: Another Adventure of Sherlock Holmes*. The book came into my possession by chance and already without a cover. This description is thus of its title page. Author: "A. Conan Doyle, author of the 'Adventures' and the 'Memoirs' of 'Sherlock Holmes,' 'The War in South Africa,' Etc. Etc." Publication: Leipzig, Bernhard Tauchnitz, 1902. In the right-hand corner, in blue pencil, notation to puzzle over:

35000

550

$\mu N = 1800$

The title page seems to have been torn off repeatedly and reattached using various adhesives. It is enough to flip through it to see that the entire book is held together with tape of some kind. Miraculously, no pages appear to be missing. They are certainly loose, but not to the point of flying out. The first word that crosses one's mind when looking at this book is "ratty"—then, quickly, "beyond ratty." The inside of the book is unmarked, save for the first few lines of the chapters "The Man on the Tor" and "Fixing the Nets"—evidence of a reader's struggles with the English language, each time abandoned midway. In the penultimate chapter (where the terror-monger's denouement can be found) just two words—"exceedingly" and "communicate"— were supplied with overhead translations.

Title: *Listy z Białołęki* [Letters from Bialoleka Prison]. Written by Adam Michnik. Published in Warsaw in 1982. The cover on this book is intact, but in terms of quality and color no different from its pages. So that at first glance this book also appears naked, a pamphlet rather than a book. The title is printed in ordinary, black capitals, whose irregularity suggests they were hand-drawn. In contrast to this cover font, the font inside is diminutive. The text's 32 pages had been offset from a typescript. Slipped inside this unassuming book by a previous owner: several sheets of paper that structurally do not belong. One is a political dissident's version of "Our Father," the other a prison letter typewritten on tissue-thin paper, addressing "fellow prisoners" with the words "I SHALL SCREAM." It is dated by hand *1977*—or rather misdated, as it was probably written in December 1981, at the start of Michnik's internment in Bialoleka, lasting until the general amnesty of 1984. What are the status and order of these pages? On the back cover, the original price: 50 zl.

Title: *Rok 1984* by George Orwell. Publisher: *Krąg*, Warsaw, 1982. At last a real cover, thick and coarse in texture, though again as white as a page, with plain, uneven lettering. The black image on this cover merits some description. A stenciled eye, surrounded by bricks in the shape of a shadow, a hint of an eyebrow. Inside the dilated pupil, a cut-out of a figure kneeling with its hands up. The book is a reprint from the only Polish-language edition at the time, published in Paris in 1953. It is typeset, but for this underground issue the font had been shrunk to 1–2 mm. The book itself measures a mere 14 x 4 cm. Out of its 254 pages the last 10 show signs, as does the back cover, of having been held above a candle: a large brown burn mark that diminishes before your eyes if you flip the pages as you would a flipbook. On the back comes a list of other titles in the series. Beneath the price (200 zl) a warning: "Don't speculate!"

Title: *Wielka Encyklopedia Tatrzańska* [The Great Encyclopaedia of the Tatra Mountains]. Authors: Zofia and Witold Paryscy. A limited edition of a superb 1500-page mountaineering classic, it is the only hide-bound volume I own. The cover is chestnut leather with four ribs across the spine. Tooled lettering on the front, on the back a folk motif, such as can still be found embroidered on the festive trousers of Tatra natives. Upon purchase the tome was in pristine condition, apparently never opened. I could not bring myself to "deflower" it without ceremony. When I finally did, I found a dried grayish plant pressed between its pages, beside the entry on *Leontopodium alpinum*—where an illustration was wanting.

I left it there, of course, thinking to supplement the rest with such content. And as I turned over its leaves, the encyclopedia revealed some of its mysteries. There was once a stretch of grassland called *Pisana Hala* (Written Pasture), whose name, of untraceable origins, had long preceded the inscriptions shepherds and amateur mountaineers would leave there in the early 1800s. I have passed over the spot many times but read nothing in it; not a trace seemed to remain of this legendary pastoral, this book of the mountains. *Implicitus est liber*. Certain writings remain hermetic even as they unfold before and beneath one like landscapes. Certain books remain shut even as they open onto other books buried within them . . . Here I find myself thinking about books again, yet again about books with equal compulsion. As though all mental paths led only to the one place, and vanished there.

F. Wren

(11.01.07)

In my previous note, what I did was I got carried away. I have no library, and of course no trace of the vast library I was describing. I wish I had many, but have only a few, books. Still a few left—and I am poor enough not to own any! I sometimes imagine I have more than I do, hyperbole on that front comes easily to me, I partly grew up in a house full of books. Definitely a *literary* household; no *scientific* household would let its children ride an abacus, that elementary tool of scientific upbringing, whose counting beads, however, became wheels in our *literary* lessons, giving as much stability but more speed than tracks on a tank, and almost absolute stability and speed for the uneven floorboards with which we were contending. Definitely a "haunted" house: creaking floors, old books, and so much time residue. The living room was called *paradiso*, the study *purgatorio*, the airless sleeping den *inferno*. The reproduction of a painting with a (deceptively) innocent title hung there and emanated a hellish (not a comforting) warmth.

Roasted (After the Bath)

The street I live on nowadays meets the northwest corner of the Provincial Lunatic Asylum. Through my window I can clearly see the asylum grounds. An iron fence used to separate them from the street, but now the grounds lie pretty much exposed, which gives someone looking in more insight into the workings of this asylum. I think back: a psychiatrist is making the rounds to see how the inmates building the wall are getting on. The inmates are occupied with building a wall around the asylum compound, standing with their bricks and their mortar and their trowels, standing (and supposedly working) *within* the asylum complex. Building this wall around themselves, for the lunatic asylum, but actually destroying walls within themselves. That is the idea. *Das Abgesteckte muß sogleich geraten . . .*[2] *What is on your mind today?* asks the doctor. "Old summers, old summer days . . ." *And what's on your mind?* "Two concentric circles, like eyes—my paranoia, doctor." *Very interesting. And what's on yours?* "They killed me." *Who killed you?* "They did." *Are you sure?* "Am I sure?!" *And on yours?* "The Face of Primal Terror. Look!" *I see.* "A fence . . . or a mesh . . . or a net." *And what about yours?* "This is a PSYCHIAT-RIC HOSPITAL, is it not? Or is this a MENTAL ASYLUM? Am I a PSYCHIATRIC PATIENT or am I a MENTAL CASE?" *Above all, my friend, you are in good hands. And how about yourself?* "Anno Domini 1884." *But that was five years ago. Why not think of the future instead? And what's on* your *mind?* "DON'T." *Alright, I won't. And you, what about you?* "Mind fatigue. Mind fatigue, that is all." *Good. Very good* (thinks or says the doctor). This wall has been very much on his mind. Is it working out and is it therapeutic. If it is working out, it must be therapeutic. If it is therapeutic then it must be working. He came out here to see if it was working. And it appears to be. *Laßt glücklich schauen, was ich kühn ersann . . .*[3] Where there's work, there is no folly. Now he can put it out of his mind. He exchanges a few words about the weather with the controller and is on his way

---

[2] "What has been staked out must at once be made" (Goethe, *Faust, pt. II*).
[3] "Let happy eyes behold my daring plan."

again, leaving the inmates to their bricklaying and to themselves. The controller's back is turned. But his hand is always on the metal box, ready to report troublemakers and idlers. These inscriptions all over the new wall—are they part of the therapy? The brick dust and the mortar are all over everyone's overalls. They are laughing and joking, they are agape with fear. Someone is practicing their penmanship, and someone is writing (across twelve bricks) a letter home: XXXXXXXXXXXXXXXXXXXXXXXXXXXXXX.

The sun is a menace, but someone draws the sun (taming the sun). Sleeves are not food, but someone chews on his sleeves (taming himself). They know how society looks, how a wall looks. They know full well how bricklayers work, they want to do as the bricklayers do when they are building. Some minds work fast, some hands work slow, but all of them are at work. A freezing morning, or else a sweltering afternoon. This is what I saw as I walked along the brick wall. I saw them, or thought I saw them, but I did not hear them. I was out of earshot, too removed (in time) to catch anything. It is said "walls have ears" when they only have eyes. And what they see is not therapy but vandalism (THERAPY-VANDALISM), not work but abuse (WORK-ABUSE), and WRITING-CURE scratched out all over. Did they know what ailed them? Did the writing cure?

The whole work, Dr. Nettle, is driving me up the wall. The work behind me as much as the work ahead of me is infinitely aggravating to think about. I don't exactly know what brain aneurysm is, but I feel that it is giving me a mind-numbing aneurysm of the brain. Yes, why is it I came to see you . . .? Ah, mine is a case of a difficult text and you specialize in such cases. It gets even more complicated. These papers I brought to show you, which I put before you, expose my neuralgic points. They expose what is most aggravating to me, and may be difficult to read on that account. People disappear, for instance, and people die without a trace. They grow up leaving behind traces, they mature and leave behind even more of them, some traces retracing the old "errors" of youth, etc., and so throughout their lives they mark up the territory in which they move with untold traces unique to them or their type. But—and this is

the funny and confusing part, equal parts funny and confusing—
suddenly they slip away and leave not a clue. They disappear completely. They may or may not be dead, but something tells us they've
met with misfortune and were done for. If they even have a grave, it
is unmarked. You can never properly bury and mourn them: there is
no end to their dead effects. Foremost among my aggravations is this
disappearance of people without a trace.

But you, dear Doctor, you must be swamped with work yourself.
What is it you are working on? Still *Adolphe*? Still Stein's autobiog-
raphy? Still the I.D. fragments? Your "effing fragments," as you say.
How are your "effing fragments" coming along? A life of fragments,
your life has been so bleeding complicated and difficult. Why, Eich-
mann himself signed off on your discharge, absent-mindedly but
effectively sparing you. Your mother coupling first with your father
then with his brother: first with your father then, once he was out
of the picture (vanished, I take it, without a trace), with his brother.
That put you, you once joked, in a Hamletesque situation. Lucky
to still have a mother, but who wants a mother that turns around
and effs (then marries) the (vanished) father's brother? You had politics breathing down your neck: appalling family politics (how they
appalled you) and fierce Jewish politics (how they confused you).
Too much politics for a little boy! It was probably wisest not to get
involved, to put all of it behind you—the minuscule disasters and the
capital disasters—and to observe the fallout from a distance through
endless inquests, murders, arrests, and trials.

Did you know I also grew up to politics (lowercase *p* family politics and uppercase *P* national politics)? The first was always in the
forefront and occupied only the forefront of my mind (which is a
shallow place). The second was in the background, continually at
the back of my mind. For that reason alone my notion of *Politics* was
exactly like my notion of *ghosts*. Although in 1981–84 I sensed the
reality of this ghostly world of political struggle, I was completely
in the dark about it. The strikes, the blue Nysa vans, the vows of
silence—tolling church bells, wailing sirens, solemn processions—
they were ubiquitous symbols of some spectral struggle. This photograph of me taken against the background of a *Lech Wałęsa affiche* is
actually a photograph of Wałęsa against an image of the times. This is
what I mean. The two of us standing in the *inferno*, Walesa looming
large within the *paradiso*.

"They fuck you up, your mom and dad"—the incisive opening to an otherwise forgettable poem. Except that I never believed even that line, which for most people is the refrain of an irreverent personal gospel, bearing the "good news" that they failed for extraneous reasons, that their failure was not of their own doing or non-doing. I never believed that excuse even for a minute. I do not think my parents' neuroses, their extreme character flaws that prevented them from cohering and ever reconciling, had been inflicted on me against my will (before I was conscious enough to rebel against them, as I later did). No, it was rather the subliminal *appeal* of these negative qualities, undeniably loathsome yet most attractive, simultaneously their worst character flaws and their strongest character traits—the pinnacles of their respective strengths of character, their worldly-wise tenacity and intransigence, their exacting natures (each exacting in its own way), and above all their inability to discipline my—their only child's—unruly conduct, the extremes of my budding force of character, due to their belief in my right to self-determination, which could transform them into *freedom-lovers* for my sake, into patrons of the questing spirit. Fundamentally, of course, this was nothing but insecure affectation, utterly unconvincing, or else simple negligence, but ostensibly I was never a liability to them (unlike many other only children) but their most *liberal product*, most precious and unique thing they engendered together; my very existence fed their illusions of being capable of selfless beneficence and magnanimity. Meanwhile, day in day out, there was nothing more important to them than work: the self-contained kind of work one performs in the nook of an office and forgets about on the way home. Not an expansive occupation by any stretch of the imagination—of the sort that takes you places emotionally and intellectually foreign. You can't expect much from a nail merchant (father) and a cardboard merchant (mother), and previously a wire merchant (father) and a textile merchant (mother). You cannot count on folks with a mercantile bias for a good upbringing. No books in our house either. But, in fairness, they neither joined nor signed. If I were to give their politics a name, it would be *isolationist nuclear-family politics*. My difficulties and galloping insubordination, my dysfunction, rivaled for attention with the evening news on Channel 1 or the American film on Channel 2. I sensed I was growing up without being brought up, and that, much as this situation was liberating, it also impoverished me, driving me to seek allies in surrogate families, to room with friends whose home-life was more congenial, whose parents were more alert instead of sleepwalking through life, and I slept and ate better at these houses, and generally felt better—so the inevitable return home was a return to solitary confinement, driving me to distraction.

I don't (to go about this differently) have the sterling personal history of a writer. Everything conspired against my writing, especially my love of drawing and painting, my early hatred of books, my ingrained contrariness towards everything done "for my own good," and (last, not least) my complete contempt for "high culture" right up to late adolescence. So I am an anti-model in almost every respect for aspiring writers. Do as I did and you may end up illiterate, and if in spite of this you *dare* write, you shall not merely fail but fail most miserably. Do as I did and you'll go straight from self-styled *poète maudit* to *poète manqué*. You think you can overcome the greatest writerly obstacles when you *choose* to overcome them and when the time is ripe for such fantastic overcoming; you think this and pile even more in your way; and when at last you do, so to speak, *choose* to overcome what needs overcoming—namely your total literary ineptitude—it is plainly too late; and your trying nonetheless makes you a laughing stock, even when no-one cares to laugh at you and you have to settle for being of such uncharismatic, tedious stock that you can't possibly make anyone laugh at your failure or show you some throwaway sympathy (though they're all likely hopeless cases themselves). That in spite of this I did not succumb to my circumstances was a miracle.

I *got at* literature and literary writing in a completely organic way but crabwise, not only because I did it against the advice of my elders and my own better judgment, but also because I did so while looking askance at literature. One could almost say I *backed into* literature and into writing, having initially set out on quite another path, then crossed over to the scholarly path, which seemed most promising. (The academic track, the *academic racetrack*, was of course nothing it promised to be; in the long run, the writing scholar was better off elsewhere, if the teaching scholar has become a menial, underpaid clerk. The writing-teaching scholars "of old" are a fiction in their thirties, a mirage in their forties, and only in their fifties a *sort of* fact.) It was just like me to take up writing literature *immediately after* crossing out the possibility of a "literary career" with its nauseating self-promotion and disingenuous accolades, and to take it up *whilst* on a steady diet of self-doubt in all my scholastic endeavors. But it is typical for difficult, headstrong characters like mine to turn around and pursue what they resolved not to pursue due to innate limitations. So, in a manner of speaking, I began and continue writing not *from* and *for* myself but *against* myself (against my difficult character, innate limitations and bad habits). So it is not a stretch to say that by writing I am effecting my own undoing. But an easy text is no match for a difficult character like mine. Only a difficult text. As far as I am concerned, I've read just enough to appreciate a difficult text, which most literate people understandably stay away from, because it cannot give them any pleasure but becomes instead a miniature torture mechanism concealed between some pasteboard. A difficult text can be hard to write and enjoy, but a difficult character is hard to undo.

Writing cannot resurrect a dead father or mother, neither of whom lived in fact beyond the moment of our conception. They took shape only to disperse like clouds. We are left in the hands of legal guardians; we have a so-called biological father and mother but are orphans nonetheless. Out of this sense of abandonment and loss some (not I) spin a myth of self-creation, others (not I) a myth of self-destruction, and still others are rent by these two myths in dramatic ways.

Limpid, playful and defenseless, words gush out with no parents to protect them. Not always wantonly begotten, but invariably orphaned once born. Once born, twice forgotten. On the one hand, we are pregnant with a book. What we really want is to get it (the work) out of our system, but of course we are not in complete control of our *mental* system. The system decides if and when it (the book) gets out. On the other hand, one is felled by book-writing as by an illness. One must submit to it, to let the illness run its course and hopefully drain itself before the book's completion. Resisting writing is like purging, vomiting, and bloodletting—woefully *medieval* cures against the mental disease called a book and the development of this disease. If you must resist, resist not writing but the book—the *physical* manifestation of the book.

The trouble is, dear Doctor, I feel emptier and emptier inside. Hour thirteen is certainly now. I have cluster headaches and pain on my mind. These constant and severe headaches are *besetting* my thoughts. The euphoria I once had is gone. Something tells me my reader is losing interest. The thought that he might be losing interest keeps me up at night. He might be losing it because he is reading a text that is difficult and not compelling enough (I am sick with worry that he does not find it compelling). He might be losing interest because he does not know who is writing to him. But what does it matter who is writing? He might want me to reveal myself and get the *charade* over with. *Reveal yourself and get it over with!* Revelation would mean the end of writing, so how can I reveal myself? I'm afraid I'm not as content with myself as I used to be. I have been trying to relieve myself of that fear and to revive myself—because that euphoria is very much *me* (I have this kind of all-natural euphoria often). But my musings and my notes haven't revived it. I am now always in a low mood. Doctor: you must have something for this. I need to go on with the book. Perhaps to make the headway I did I went astray. On the other hand, I have followed the map very closely. Call me a literary fool—for that is what I think I am, in my heart of hearts—*a literary lunatic*. Not a regular fool, not a regular lunatic. In that (regular) respect I am quite sane. You see, *my writing* is my lunacy, not me. My notes are *literary* follies—and those aren't certifiable.

F. Wren

Permission

(11.14.07)

Some convergences of illness and solitude, of solitude and hypertension, leave no doubt as to the naturally restorative power of writing. The impetus to write separates solitude from illness, and illness from distress, and in no time consciousness runs freely again. Like that time just past, or still at the peak of, my crisis—who can really say if I was still at the peak or if I had come down somewhat, and it were merely the after-effects, fatigue and mounting depression, that accompanied me on that off-season trip with my mother (obliging because she saw me so seldom and I seemed unwell)— seven hours' drive south from Warsaw, through Cracow, down the nearly empty (in this time of year) *Zakopianka* motorway to Zakopane[4] itself—which, I swore throughout, was not my destination but a mere orientation-stop; then, having checked into one of those inns that exude a pungent odor of disinfectants (filling your head with imagined filth), driving briefly around the area before nightfall in search of a place that lived up to my ideal of perfect and total isolation, my "mountain retreat," but finding only cheap imitations; setting out, thus, immediately after breakfast the next day to cruise through Murzasikhle, Glodovka, Male Tsikhe, to then plunge deeper into the Tatra foothills (as far as the border at Lysa Polana) by a pitted one-lane forest route, on the lookout for secluded resorts that had seen their heyday and were now in a state of ambient neglect, but again finding none to match such criteria; so back again, along winding and branching roads until they proved impassable, on through Jashchurovka, Cyrhla in the early afternoon, to finally, after a light dinner, negotiate the vertiginous arm of Mt. Gubalovka (sheltering Zakopane from the northwest) and, after several off-season enquiries at various shuttered domiciles, settle on a house on the steeper slope

---

[4] Döblin's xenophobic depiction of Zakopane in *Journey to Poland* (1925) spoiled it for me—though I barely recognized it. Only to Karl May's near-contemporaries could the Tatra highlanders resemble Indians.

dusted by May snow. It was in one of these illegally built houses (as I was later told) offering an unobstructed view of the Tatra panorama that I made my temporary home, without having to *settle* for anything, since it was really the best of both worlds—*solitude* and *society* (with just the right proportions of hostly warmth and unconcern)—at the peak of a three-storey log house, where besides my room (a garret no bigger than three by three, with a small window in the shape of a triangle) were two frigid chambers facing east and west. In that undersized room I slept for all of three weeks. The triangular view on the jagged summits engrossed me for ages, especially at daybreak, when a heavy mist spread over the rolling meadows, and on afternoons when the sky hung low with precipitation. I gazed out at those nameless crags until condensation from my breath obscured them from me. Lying on my bed, atop the sleeping house and sleeping town below, I often felt—how shall I put it—metaphysical. And on some days the window put me in mind of God. Then there were agonizing nights when I regretted having missed the evening express to Warsaw. With the room bright, the black triangle confronted me with my own reflection. At such altitudes—the only lights around deep in a valley, shimmering like embers or fallen stars—night can still throw you back upon yourself. It occurred to me at one time that the narrow closet behind my door, which stood empty, was exactly the size of a coffin—and if I stood in it once or twice, my arms down by my side, it was possibly to verify this. There were times I hardly knew what to do with myself.

Outwardly I was depressed and dejected, inwardly I was anything but, and secretly I was winding and working myself up into a manic state of awareness. As soon as I arrived, I knew I could not languish in my newfound solace; keeping to one's room with such beauty outdoors was practically impossible. (It was there and it penetrated.) As soon as I settled in, I knew it wasn't to think but to act. So on the second evening of my mountain stay I sat down on the edge of my pallet, took out a notebook I bought for throwaway thoughts, and began writing—what, I couldn't tell you, because I no longer remember—as a work it was inconsequential, but the activity itself brought instant relief. There I was (a mere two days ago) thinking myself a lame duck! Here I am, on day two, already feeling and getting better (I thought this on the morning of day three, not having slept a wink the previous night). In that one sitting I filled countless pages with indecipherable scribble. I noticed it helped me to become absorbed in something self-forgetfully—after so much time spent thinking only of myself and my physical and mental decline, I was definitely on the mend. And all I was doing was writing! But it was a somnambulist's script, from impulse, motivated by intuition and emotion instead of deliberation (had thought entered into it, it would have set back my recovery). Days and nights followed one another in this fugue as I gave myself over to my task, whose purpose was not a piece of literature but peace of mind. Instead of sacrificing my health to writing, I sacrificed my writing to health. I set my own hours as the rhythm of the work, my "alpine remedy," dictated. A week or so later, my momentum flagging, I was back on my feet. I had gained more than I had lost in that episode given over to handwriting; I had broken the spell of illness and felt a general sense of accomplishment, despite having written nothing of note. I had perhaps turned my fate around, or perhaps it was all on the cards before I got there.

Next thing I knew I was marching with my host's children up and down the mountain. The walks up, like the walks down, resembled *partituras* engraved in the landscape.

On the way down the mountain one passed by the apiary, the penned rabbits, and, after some dozen footbridges (thrown over chasms and sliding mud), a goat chained to a sward; but on the way up the mountain, taking a different route, one passed shepherds with their sheepdogs and droves of sheep; and the sand-hill one passed on the descent and ascent alike—a huge mound of sand dumped beside cement blocks, where the landscape was particularly desiccated. The long log cabin next to it the children called *evil*, though I never got to the bottom of why. It was abandoned and gave off the smell of rot. Some minutes later, one could already glimpse a familiar lean-to and the host's heifer through the thinning trees. The mountain's gradient varied every few hundred steps, as one crossed a cultivated patch or a fir woods riven with gorges.

Apart from these regular treks to and from Zakopane (often with only my old Olympus for a companion), I was out and about most of the day, heedless of the time, invigorated by the wind and the drizzle. I also took brisk walks along the flat ridge of the mountain: past the wooden chapel, the kiosk, the tavern, the deserted funicular station, the restaurant and terrace *Morskie Oko*, the boarded-up souvenir shacks. A few days before I left, unseen, I threw the pages I had inked into a creek by Butorov.

In those days I had no hopes other than convalescing in solitude; what I received exceeded those hopes. In retrospect, of course, it was a peculiar holiday: devoted to solitude after a solitary year abroad. As I was leaving for the station, the *halny* wind had passed over the bald heights to the nether hills, touching off a climatic depression. A good time to come down from my mountain.

F. Wren

(11.22.07)

One starts low and writes upwards. To write a book is to hike up a mountain, then to hike down it—perhaps the more grueling being this downward hike, this writing downhill. But one does not hike up just to hike down again; there is the summit, the point of the entire hike. One approaches this uppermost point knowing, or sensing, that it is also the point of *crisis* (dramatically, not morally, speaking): the peak of an approaching crisis, towards which one has been advancing the whole time one was thinking of the peak and looking forward to the breathtaking view from there. And a crisis in writing—the highest point it will achieve—is a book's potential demise. We falter before taking the last measured step that will put us on the summit because it may simultaneously put us over the edge—nullify what lies below, obliterate the countless steps already taken. Jacques Derrida's handling of this simple observation turns it into poetic truth: "the tip of the summit (the peak) belongs to another order than that of the summit; the highest is therefore contrary to or other than what it surpasses; it is higher than the height of the most high."

But what's this now? *Not yet.* The peak has come into view, but not in its entirety (only the lower part of it is). It is clearly visible, therefore not arbitrary. The crisis it denotes is the highest of self-critical points: testing the ambit of one's writing/passion/solitude, configuring the *beyond* for all three. What better place to launch yourself into the beyond than from the acme of your achievement? At that moment, it becomes a question of launching yourself beyond-and-up or beyond-and-down—of flying or falling. And of apostrophes ('): a self-styled genius's flight/fall or a self-styled nobody's flight/fall. And of exclamations (!). On the peak I can find and think many things, just not the book. I couldn't think, for example: "What is this I'm writing? Is it a book? Can I finish this book? Can it be finished?" Those are questions one asks on one's ascent or descent, never on the top. Other questions and observations are the signage of crisis. (For example, the altophobic "How does one get down from here? I will never come down"; or the amnesiac "How did I ever get this high? What am I doing here?"; or the megalomaniacal "I'm in my rightful place. I might just stay here indefinitely"; or the neurotic "Only failure awaits me if I keep going. I'll be exposed for the fraud that I am"; or, lastly, the suicidal "Time to jump off this cliff!"). It's like this: fear grips us when it's time to start our descent, which either way begins atop. We are speechless again. We imagine ourselves buried beneath this half-formed mountain of words we have scaled.

If you climb pro forma, the peak is a rest-stop, an intermission. But as a real climber, reaching it you come face to face with a bewildering silence. Up there, despite all your elation, you come upon deepest doubt. A deep disorientation. Approaching it, writers are no longer sure anyone will listen to them; once there, they cannot even formulate a word. No more can they tell where the silence is coming from. I know I am near that point—the loftiest turning point—when I no longer believe you are there. It could be that someone else is there, just not you. I am beginning to think: my highest standard has forsaken me. This experimenting of mine differs from writing an ordinary book only in the timing, intensity, and distribution of that tension between me and the reader, in whose boots I hike part of the time.

But what's this? Am I writing a book now, most definitely? I am writing, and what I know about writing *comes into play*—what I know of books comes into play, too—but whether this work shapes itself into a work, and these notes transform themselves into a book is not (particularly) up to me. In some sense, I am too caught up in the work. I'm getting both my hands dirty. To paraphrase a line from a great book, all play has the character of a work, not just of energy. But what kind of work obtains from this *ludic undertaking*—erotic or intellectual? Energy is always expended; it is a question merely of its excess or deficiency. Will the work overflow with or lack vivacity? One must hold it in reserve to continue, to feel that continuing is possible. But reserves are not enough. One must pull out the plan again, the map, the schedule: get to the top and come down on the other side. Consider the compass, the sun, the lie of the land, study the legend of the map. My objective always included writing up everything connected with this writing, this passion, this solitude. Nothing I have noted up to this point is part of some extemporization or idiosyncratic way to kill time (yours, mine). I have (in fact) climbed a long way, following a carefully drawn-up plan. I now see only the summit; everything beneath is engulfed by clouds. I think: turn back now and you are petrified.

This work is a structure without foundations.

The climax affords a holiday only to exalted cretins. They stand basking in unfiltered sunrays and are damaged by them. Such ruthless exposure to the sun adumbrates your mind within moments (it allegedly works like an aphrodisiac). Do you see these wormholes? If you developed an image of my mind in a darkroom, you would see them, surrounded by dead gray matter: tunnels eaten away by maggots multiplying rapidly in the sunshine. You can thread queer and foreign ideas through them and I wouldn't notice. They are and are not part of my brain; they are unoccluded (if convoluted) passages through it. If you lit a light bulb beside the amygdala, light would stream forth as from a *jack-o-lantern*—but this would not prove my brilliance, merely the eternal brilliance of light.

Since I wouldn't be able to ask myself later, I might as well ask myself now, when I am in command of speech. (This is a calibration.) Can I give myself up without giving up the work (writing)? Can I give up the book (the work) when I am finished with it (or it with me)? Yes, a book *is* underway. And if it is, it must end and be finished, and if it ends, I must wash my hands of it, and if I do (remove it like grime from overworked hands), I will have given it up. But to be given up, this so-called finished book must amount to nothing, *nothing*—in any case, not to a book, even if it eventually takes that shape. This is another way of saying that it must fail as a book, become unrecognizable in its appearance as a book.

It is a vicious circle. I commit this work serially, and it is an indecent and arrested work. Each time I stop I interrogate and incriminate myself, blackmail myself with its secret. I turn suspect, criminal, and victim. I respond (always the same response): *This is what it is, precisely not what it seems*, pointing to the invariably half-empty, half-filled sheet in front of me which has, meanwhile, taken on the treacherous appearance of a book, a screaming and burning book—like hellfire and the holy writ thrown together. I am the last to say, with Prospero's famous reluctance, "This thing of darkness I acknowledge mine." Am I not giving a damning testimony through my actions, my going after and manipulating the word? If you must know, I am set to work by it; this writing is my personal slave-driver. I submit to it of my own accord, I imagine myself its accomplice, though I also denounce it. I am, after all, still on this side of the law. Yet under no condition would I hand over my own flesh and blood. I am too hung-up on it. It is at heart a fugitive work, pursued for transgression and sentenced in *absentia* to oblivion. But the lunatic work may in the end clear itself in your eyes, ending up beyond (not before!) the law. It might free itself from guilt, doubt, and confusion—not, however, through full disclosure, not through short shrift before execution, not in belated triumph of certainty and clarity. To let it fall wholly outside the framework of *conviction*—for some writers, that is a risk remarkably worth taking. . . A work on the run escapes by voiding (not clearing!) its conscience, by *making the obscurity of language correspond to the clarity of things*. To transgress is sometimes to transcend the chiaroscuro of an open book.

F. Wren

(12.11.07)

I write to you as though I were speaking to you. This speech is an abstraction and a sensation. (I am) a disembodied voice feeding into your ear. I hear myself inside the mask I wear and hide behind. Behind a ritual mask I speak what I cannot openly express. There is nothing quite like the masked performance in which the performer suppresses their fear, yet still it lingers in the crevices of their features and clings to their fingertips. Though exorcized like a malevolent spirit, the fear is palpable and part of a sublime atmosphere.

There are times I'm overcome with sadness at being confined to writing—to masking an inner speech that is ordinary and must reach you transformed. I identify with the mask, or a series of masks, created for speaking to you, and, when I do speak, I adapt myself to their range of expression. Each one is a container for my voice, which escapes as through a whistle. Each one contains my voice differently, letting it out as a different sound. This may be the only way to think of this writing. For such writing, the way of a mask may be the only way. "A mask is not primarily what it represents but what it transforms, that is to say, what it *chooses* not to represent. Like a myth, a mask denies as much as it affirms. It is not made solely of what it says or thinks it is saying, but of what it excludes." So it is with masked speech—audible on the inside, then, through the writing, transformed. I sit propped up on an elbow (one of many props in this unrehearsed performance), recalling an arrangement with masks, of masks, and about masks, their inaudible voices.

Scene: American museum, permanent exhibit on the Northwest Coast Indians. "This place," wrote Claude Lévi-Strauss over six decades ago, "on which outmoded but singularly effective museographic methods have conferred the additional allurements of the chiaroscuro of caves and the tottering heap of lost treasures, may be seen daily from ten to five o'clock . . ." Today, the museum's oldest hall is essentially what it was back then, except comparatively more outmoded, neglected, and elusive. Modernization, sweeping through the more popular exhibits, has left it virtually untouched. As the aboriginal cultures—from which the artifacts gathered here derive—reclaim their heritage, this colonial storehouse loses its "archaic" aura and appears eerily out of place. Two recent calendars featuring wooden masks from the collection bear out, I think, this state of affairs, as does the number (scarcely worth mentioning) of visitors to pass through the hall during my time there. The objects that caught my attention were the so-called Speaker and Echo masks, which at one time played a role in the potlatch, or giving feast, among the indigenous peoples of the coastal Northwest: the Kwakiutl (whose "unbridled imagination" can be seen in "stupefying orgies of form and color"), the Nuxalk ("whose masks affect a stately style"), the Heiltsuk, and the Tlingit (whose carvings are "of subtle and poetic inspiration"). The design of these two personae—the Speaker, who praised, and the Echo, a spirit or ghost imitating human and animal voices—was limited if one compared them to the elaborateness, whimsicality, and vibrant pigments of "transformation" masks, masks with names like Wild Man of the Woods, Cannibal, Octopus, Wasp, Bull's Head, or Bear's Knee Cap, and various beaked, finned, and snouted visors and headdresses with hair made of wild grasses, feathers, patches of fur, or strips of leather. The mask of the *Listener* (or *Imitator*)—which in my ignorance I took to complement the other two—made a bizarre impression with its whitewashed wood and protruding, cylindrical eyes that seemed to rotate in their orbits, suggesting a gaze at once transfixed and transfixing.

But the masks that held me captive sported a unique feature: detachable mouths. On one interpretation, at one time, these mouthpieces of diverse shapes were to be mimicked by the mouths of watchers. On another, they assisted the performer in modulating his speech, song, and dance. The open mouth (sometimes forming an O) allowed the voice to pass through freely; the sealed mouth, often with clenched teeth, would have muffled it. Save for the taut or rictal mouths of the Nuxalk Echo, the lips of all were painted a delectable reddish color, which lent them a lifelike expression. Some seemed to be pulling faces.

The Indian exposition exceeds masks—but it is the masks that draw one into the mythical worldview of their creators. The variety of objects here assembled is staggering. Totemic sculptures, flush against the columns of the main aisle, no longer compete for prominence with the thirty-foot Haida canoe that once stood in its centre; dusty ceremonial rattles, costumes, and armor crowd together behind glass; tools, ornaments, and coppers are everywhere displayed to advantage. They send the anthropologist into raptures:

> From one showcase to the other, from one object to the next, from one corner to another within the same object sometimes, it is as if one were transported from Egypt to twelfth-century France, from the Sassanids to the merry-go-rounds of suburban amusement parks, from the palace of Versailles, with its arrogant emphasis on crests and trophies, its almost shameless recourse to plastic metaphor and allegory, to the forests of the Congo.

It is a trance that renders topsy-turvy many familiar hierarchies. After hours of scrutiny, one's head begins reeling with human-animal hybrids and unsystematizable transformations. I am surely not alone with the creeping sense that they remain opaque and mute to the most knowledgeable visitor, but as one turns away resume their age-old colloquies. How long will they repose here, seemingly outside time, to stir the imagination?

After leaving the museum, feeling out of sorts, I walk through the park. For fully an hour I stand watching a carousel in motion, the force of revolution bearing up the horses and garlands, casting its zoo- and phytomorphic spell upon the riders. Enveloped by whirling smudges of color, by tunes merging with laughter—from this contagious joy, this vicarious abandon, my spirits improve. I withdraw and meander through the park until dusk. On the one hand, I think (inconclusively) of the carvers and painters of the carousel's majestic steeds, teeth bared and hooves kicking up the air behind them, on the other, of the carvers and painters of native masks, tongues lolling, a raven's beak opening onto a human face. . .

As you can see, having turned the corner somehow, I go on. Just as I had written myself into a crisis before, I have now written myself out of it. The book about masks, the very ones I set out to see, fell into my hands for the very purpose of dispelling my fears. A sick individual stands on crutches—literally or when on his medication—and a writer relies on another's book to give him courage and strength. Borrowing them from others until he can stand on his own. In situations where the odds rising against us seem insurmountable, we borrow what we need, if it is on hand, and simply keep going. These borrowed words and thoughts—without them a book, any book, would be unsupportable. And why not make this explicit? Because it is an insult to genius?! I have barely moved from the spot, I am still much too weak, but I have already insulted genius, and that is a positive development. Just recently, you see, I fell foul of my own judgment—my harsh dismissal of this work, giving me leave to abort it. I have not yet fully recovered, have not therefore recovered the resolve for continuing such a work as this: a work performed while being written. To continue working under such pressure, that is, to continue at once with a script and a performance, requires ever greater investment and concentration of energy.

I take my last principle from a people without writing. As *masked speech*, writing is a transformation of speech—of incoherent, ordinary speech. I am committed to signs that reveal just as much as they conceal. Thus I am trapped within a maze of seemingly insoluble contradictions, every motif prone to bifurcate at some point, taking me down tortuous paths. Transgression or discretion. Deception or honesty. Obscurity or clarity. Speech or writing. Mouths or eyes. I speak to the absence of you, echoing your silence.

Fearn Wren

(12.23.07)

Too much snow and a white fairytale turns into a white nightmare. We can no longer distinguish the contours of things we are used to seeing—nothing outside of our snowed-in dwelling seems to exist, but reveals only fragments of itself, forcing us to infer its full shape or draw it from memory (too often inaccurate). So that a world snowed under, with snowdrifts like mountain ranges along every street, capping roofs, blanketing yards and walkways, becomes a memory of a world that has disappeared.

With such whiteness stretched out before you, confining as much as releasing you from duties and obligations, you might ask yourself whether the world as you remember it has lost only some or all of its meaning, whether *world* wasn't merely a fancy word for meaninglessness. A whiteness so white that even it ceases to exist, and you with it. As nature reasserts itself where it was all but stamped out, the world as you know it might strike you as a crude invention. On this great canvas, you start to re-invent the world in keeping with your own taste, and for the first time perhaps concede the necessity of imperfection. You hope that the next time you see it the world will be different, the myriad activities people engage in will have replenished their meaning and gained more purchase on your life, while you will realize they are in fact essential. Snow has draped everything so totally overnight that you think you may have woken up to another dream—show me a man who wouldn't wish for a *scene change* beneath this curtain. But the clarity outside is merely a blindfold. You know that the old and buried world (you wish it were buried) is merely hibernating, or another such world hatching underneath. Right now, you imagine, people are busy making plans just like before or maybe more so, telephoning each other, keeping in touch through thick and thin, and no-one wishes this bleakness on the world, no-one sees things the way you do, no-one wallows in the deplorable state of that world. Instead of feeling threatened and helpless as children, they are *taking advantage* of nature, reveling in it, marveling at it—their glee and good sense equally childlike. You feel this episode—for that is what it is (the snowplows are already on their way)—is to no avail. Everyone loves the white landscape for its purity, for briefly "erasing" all squalor, but they are addicted to squalor, unwilling to part with it, they wouldn't dream of going that far. Meanwhile, you still imagine yourself a purist.

Here is not the immaculate whiteness of the Northern icecaps, but the *white blight* of metropolitan fringes. And the solitude that agrees with it is also not Northern: not a collective sense of isolation on the arctic frontier, affecting a group of people who represent (or think they represent) Humanity against the frozen bosom of Nature. It is, on the contrary, the individual (and no less paradoxical) solitude of urban peripheries. It closes in on you in an entirely different way. These snow-clad urban peripheries, cold and quiet now beyond belief, are a more hostile place than that waste in the mythic North where land becomes sky.

The city dispenses both kinds of solitude: the one you don't want, the sense of abandonment that strikes only when you are near a great many people who know nothing of your need for them, and which becomes a terminal illness, and the other one, the solitude you seek out in the midst of people and actually enjoy. A city's outskirts are the ideal playground for the first, the wretched lonesomeness. Throw a snowstorm into the mix and you feel isolated, not a soul in the world aware of your existence. (Even without a storm, in every so-called open city half the residents are shut-ins.) As for the second kind of solitude, it can be found in the city centre. It was Baudelaire who first sketched its poetics:

[E]njoying a crowd is an art; and only he can relish a debauch of vitality at the expense of the human species, on whom, in his cradle, a fairy has bestowed the love of masks and masquerading, the hate of home, and the passion for roaming. Multitude, solitude: identical terms, and interchangeable by the active and fertile poet.

The man who is unable to people his solitude is equally unable to be alone in a bustling crowd . . . The solitary and thoughtful stroller finds a singular intoxication in this universal communion. The man who loves to lose himself in a crowd enjoys feverish delights that the egoist locked up in himself as in a box, and the slothful man like a mollusk in his shell, will be eternally deprived of. ["Crowds"]

For Baudelaire, the marketplace, the street, the fair were ideal places for such solitary pursuits—let's agree, selfish pursuits of solitude, in which fellowship plays no part. Nietzsche dismissed them as absurd: Where solitude endeth, there beginneth the market-place . . . Away from the market-place and from fame taketh place all that is great: away from the market-place and from fame have ever dwelt the devisers of new values . . . Flee, my friend, into thy solitude: I see thee stung all over by the poisonous flies! . . . [I]t is not thy lot to be a fly-flap. [*Thus Spake Zarathustra*]

One guesses that, whether real or imaginary, crowds are anathema to such solitude; a *peopled* solitude is nothing more than a market-place of the mind. Baudelaire's solitary of crowds (thriving, disorienting, orgiastic) remains himself or becomes another at will in his hysterical search for universal communion. Yet beneath this conceit of pure volition he wants nothing more than to be left to himself without being left alone. He claims to need no-one for his happiness when in fact he needs them all, and up close! And while he is charitable— Baudelaire refers to the poet's charity towards strangers, a generosity of feeling he deems more ineffable than love itself—the foundation of this charity (and all charity) is giving away what we can do without. There he roams, over-above the crowd, the residual Romantic, the haughty poetic genius! How he feeds on our warmth and seeks redemption in numbers.

How different is the solitude of the graveyard-walker, the habitué of cemeteries (however crowded), who desires fellowship with the dead, equal amongst themselves, an imaginary fellowship across the great divide. He or she knows better than to take pride in solitude. The post-modern writer has many affinities with such a figure. He, too, seeks at once solitude and sodality with those who *are not there*. His is, through and through, a thoughtful solitude. One appreciates the intrepidness of Nietzsche's appeal if one considers that, for most, solitude becomes bearable when thought is pared to an instrumental minimum. This lower limit and minimum of solitary thinking is much like meditation; it entails forgetting about one's solitude and persisting in it on the necessity of thought itself. But the upper limit, the maximum of solitary thought, is on the cusp of questioning solitude itself and turning over to fellowship one's solitary perspective. The golden mean one strives for is a balancing act between thought of the world and the underworld, of the here and the hereafter.

One fears becoming a casualty of solitude. There is a stigma attached to the solitude-seeker; she or he is a liminal figure, existing on the margins of social life, un-forgotten, a thorn in the side of those she shuns, who want to punish her or get rid of the memory of her. A line that haunts me from one childhood story: *"I'm a lone Rock Spur,"* cried the Rock Spur to the Bottom-of-the-Sea, *"Can't you see how lonely I am?"* The rock's wish to stand out from the great mountain had been granted—but how plaintive is its solitary tone. In the end, the mountain agrees to take the breakaway rock in again. Unhappiness and guilt are wished upon those who venture solitude.

About all I could do as the blizzard ran its course is look back on everything I have written to you. A midwinter review may be a real test for a book that may have no right to exist. The first thought that came to my mind was predictably self-deprecating: what a boring and dreary idea to write a book to tell the story of that very book. No matter if it's the long or the short story, the long story made short or the short one made long, or even the so-called history of the book's conception. I would expect such a book to have nothing going for it. In many ways, re-reading it was like visiting a morgue: staring a dead thing in the face and being asked to identify and own up to it, and asking it in turn, who bore you and did your life even matter? On an ordinary day, I would not have gone through with it.

Fearn Wren

P.S. You must forgive me now for giving you this writing in a new way, restated and reframed (though still wonderfully full of gaps). You may be surprised to see it in this light. (How natural it now seems to me to write to you in earnest and candidly, without the vanity of writing.) In normal circumstances, to refuse a gift is to affront the giver; there is normally this pressure on us to accept, to take anything that comes our way without turning up our nose. But you are under no such constraint. You may casually refuse this gift and leave it unopened. With you, it has always been silence, which has many meanings. I am quite used to it by now. Perhaps it would help you to receive me if you could picture me, qua me. You could not possibly remember me. But picture me at least: a pair of eyes in a darkened auditorium.

(01.05.08)

Mobilis in mobili.

I once got about on foot all the time—there is a period, when we are young, when we cannot even walk, only run—but before long this conscious or unconscious boycott of mechanical means of travel must conflict with other, sedentary activities, which—if one is committed to them, let alone obsessed with them—begin to fill one's life to the exclusion of activities that involve and, in some sense, celebrate walking; in effect, our entire manner of living soon becomes incompatible with walking, and our stride is traded for a set of wheels or rails. Oh, we study the peripatetic philosophers and try (fail) to fathom them, we believe what we hear of the positive effects of walking on the intellect, of the Romantic charms of rural walking tours on one's sensibility, but to leave this city on foot, leave it behind and really start *walking*, would take days (we'd have to camp along the way!) The further you move from such a city after dark, the more its lustrous glory becomes evident to you. Even if this city's suburbs were to stretch on forever, their wan electric glow would pale against that of the city itself, which—as you look back on it—keeps you spellbound. I suspect everyone could name a recluse they admire and try (fail) to emulate, somebody who defied all that needed defying to cut himself loose from society. The recluse has no existence outside of his relation to society, the stranger would not exist without the well-knit community, and the traveller without those who dwell continually in one place. In the same self-evident way, the pedestrian was born of the marriage of cities and mechanical locomotion. But, despite resistance from habit, I started walking again.

I took up walking because of a chronic pain that (she promised) was amenable to this simple treatment. And, sure enough, it's long gone. I keep walking to keep it at bay. Whenever I walk in the interest of walking, I naturally become engrossed in the act itself: the sprightly, springy motion of one's limbs, the shifts of intensity, the distance one covers, the advantages of ambulation as a form of transit, and the dangers it exposes one to—very different from those faced behind a wheel. If there exists perfect harmony between walking and thinking, when neither is out of step, this must be it. One leg after the other and one thought after the other, one's footfalls timed to steps in one's cogitation, one's thoughts regulated by one's perfectly linear progression. (Not a kinetics of walking as thinking, but a concordance of feet and ideas planted on solid ground; literal and mental footholds simultaneously.) When my "walking cure" was at its most taxing, I would walk very far lost in thought without taking in any of my surroundings, only the basic and rough data about where I was and where I was headed. I have always had trouble taking in the landscape around me, obsessed as I am with moving through and past it, with making progress in my movement, with striking out towards no destination. It is much the same with writing, which tends to focus on itself once it becomes "second nature." One hopes to end up beyond the horizon, far beyond the foreseeable. One brings a provisional map only to discard it at an opportune moment. I no longer possess the map of this writing—not that there ever was a reliable map for what is practically quicksand.

One is tempted to follow even the charted and anti-pedestrian routes called freeways—the quicker to get beyond them. Last spring, I decided to pursue one such route, black as ink, running across this country. I left my purlieus and continued half-consciously for most of the afternoon, hypnotized, it seems, by the hum of fleeting vehicles. My only memory from this escapade (which I have no intention of repeating) is of the Bombardier manufacturing plant in Mirabel. I may have singled it out based on a "match" between my thoughts—which, again, had nothing to do with my surroundings—and the sight of that sprawling industrial park. In my mind I was wending my way through a kind of museum and, as I walked on, began projecting it onto Bombardier's invisible assembly lines: the planes and jets in the aircraft building, the locomotives in the railway building, snowmobiles in the snowmobile building, subway cars in the subway building, etc. At this crepuscular hour, production was probably halted and the facilities were closed. But an outsider can never tell with certainty if they are closed or open—they look closed even when they are open and, for all one knows, never close but keep on cranking out their machines after hours. If one looks around and considers the invisible landscape, a landscape's underbelly as it were, then all one sees is factories. Everywhere something is being produced. Everywhere one finds the makings of museums, and of museums of museums.

The Museum of Writing-Machines was just another fabrication. The more one pondered its exhibits, the less one understood the arcane workings of language. Each object was ostensibly there to shed light on the phenomenon of writing, on its relationship to itself and to other facets of human life. Instead (as can be expected), such systematic display of connections and relations tended to obscure rather than clarify even the simplest writing act. To give an example: *The train—the rhythm of modern prose attains the rhythm of a rumbling train, the perfect pitch of a train whistle, and the motivation of a vehicle unswerving in its approach of its destination. The writer of prose rides the Express, speeding single-mindedly past places he has never heard of. (Not that he cares.) Only the essayist can trundle along on an ordinary train, taking his time and a First Class window seat.* One thing the museum did make clear, in its characteristically elliptical fashion, was this: writing is often mechanical work, not unlike the operation of a piece of machinery. But it is no easier for being mechanical. Despite what is claimed to the contrary, everyone doubles over with writing; it is difficult and painful; our expectations and standards always outstrip our ability to actually communicate by its means. But as I moved through this indescribable "museum"—the "stations" of this mechanical "passion" of the Word, from its apotheosis to its crucifixion—my thoughts continued to dissipate, until I was no longer sure what purpose it all served, other than to dissuade me from writing. I knew I had to leave behind as fast as I could these clocks, windmills, looms, and perpetuum mobiles.

At one point I paused, being reminded of a tribute to mechanical motion, and to the blind trust and chance allied with it: a prime example of writerly obsession from a mind addicted to opiates and often decelerating, I imagine, to a snail's pace. De Quincey treats us to a minute account of a would-be accident, averted by a hair's breadth, between two horse-drawn carriages set on a collision course with each other—one of them a *mail-coach*, his favorite writing vehicle, his writing-machine. He explains its appeal, first, through its velocity, second, through the "grand effects for the eye between lamp-light and the darkness upon solitary roads," third, through the beauty of its four horses, fourth, through the presence of a "central intellect," which "in the midst of vast distances, of storms, of darkness" overcomes all obstacles, and fifth, through the grandeur of the "mail establishment." If a man running from his fate were to ask him, "'Whither can I go for shelter? Is a prison the safest retreat? Or a lunatic hospital? Or the British Museum?'" he would reply, "'Take lodgings for the next forty days on the box of his majesty's mail. Nobody can touch you there.'" That's writing for you—nobody can touch you there.

My walks seldom take me as far. My usual route is to the liquor store and back: a thirty-minute paseo through Little Portugal, past a *peixaria* whose proprietress has scales instead of skin, to the other side. I find that when one is walking and one's mind roving one ends up writing anyway (if such is one's habit); one's thoughts compose themselves into writerly thoughts, often with great panache. There is no telling what one can accomplish on a longer walk.

***

It is said that in everything we should be both near- and farsighted, but this principle has no straightforward application. For why should writing a book be short-sighted, and what should be far-sighted about jotting down notes, with little or no continuity between them? Each note going into this book seems at first a product of nearsightedness; but then there is something to be said for its being more farsighted than the book itself. Writing it is like beginning the book all over again—can one really afford to be short-sighted about such beginnings? I do not know where this book is going as a whole, but I do know where each fragment is going and where it is taking the book.

All your energy ought to be pumped into a work when progress in the work is at stake. This creates enough pressure to transmit your thoughts (I am thinking along the lines of a *pneumatic mail delivery system*). You identify yourself and your life with the work so fully that you cannot think outside it, cannot think of anything not connected with it, or think about anything without also thinking about it—even time spent away from writing or thinking about writing is time indirectly spent on the book. The so-called downtime is nothing but the gathering of momentum for the upward surge, a period of gestation for each successive stage of the book. You play a titillating *waiting-game* with the work. Or *blind man's bluff* with the work. You are completely consumed with it and, at the same time, totally inconspicuous, so that the one closest to you does not know that you are writing, or that what you are writing is book-like, and that you live by it, literally live by this book.

Anyone with any perspicacity can see there is something romantic about toiling in secrecy and obscurity, and something erotic in writing to a stranger one has no business writing to. This romance of writing, whatever form it takes, has little in common with love— only perhaps that bliss at having hit upon *les mots justes* with which one is not ashamed to address one's lover. But a true obsession is anything but romantic. One either loses oneself in it too mechanically or loses sight of the object of writing (communication, for the record). Obsession not only regenerates desire but exposes desire for what it is: self-seeking and self-perpetuating. Obsession with written work bears down singularly on the work's progress and becomes a motor for objectless desire. This work will end, I cannot say the same for my obsession with writing to you. Whatever such works I have in me I can only conceive of writing with you in mind—you'll make a writer of me yet!

For every artist, no matter how difficult, the goal is facility: a clear plateau where he or she can finally be at ease with creative expression. There are always higher planes of facility to which we can aspire. But, of course, this height of facility and clarity is tantamount to the end of art. Artistic work is naturally overshadowed by so many things. It is notoriously hard to handle—more for the artist than anyone else. It is also not without its compromises. Granted, this *giving-writing game* that I am playing with you has never been easier to play. But it's a difficult game. Your silence is not absolute. I do not really turn myself over to nothingness. I suffer less from fear and guilt of having offended than from not having pleased you enough. I retain the freedom of coming and going. Though I must return, I can do so anytime; though I must leave, I determine when, and when to leave for good. But I haven't the option of abandoning this work. I will see it through, even as this seeing-through becomes more and more difficult. If it must end, let it end with dignity. *Just not yet.*

So this work is evidence of a passion turned obsession. In my writing delirium I was *non compos mentis*; in my writing obsession I am there, but not wholly there either. It is no longer a question of calculation or spontaneity in the usual sense of these words; one is not in control in the usual sense. Obsession can strike even (especially) when one thinks one has mastered one's work. When the lifelong apprenticeship wears on, dreams of mastery spur us on. The obsessive streak in our constitution is inflamed by such confidence and acts up again and again. Obsession with a work leads us to stretch its life to the breaking point. The work is now a mere plaything of the creative/destructive possibilities of our *idée fixe*. That is why both the egomaniac and the martyr like to "let go of the reins." But—to at once clear up a potential misunderstanding—it is not a question of letting go when the mind has already ceased to obey us.

For the past week, I toyed with the idea of writing an academic paper for a conference dedicated to obsession and addiction. But can one hope to delve into obsession (and addiction) or addiction (and obsession) without yielding to it and jeopardizing analytic formulae? To "examine" obsession is always to stand outside it, too cool-headed to live it. No doubt mindful of the conundrum, the conference organizers hedgingly promised debate about *representations* of obsession and addiction for the sake of truth. They took further precaution by billing their meeting as "international and interdisciplinary" for the sake of appearances. Just don't expect this debate about "the emotional, psychological and physiological states of obsession and addiction, their causes and their consequences" to explain anything about anything. Actual obsession and addiction must be left at the door. Academic conversations are for throwing around ideas about representations, then running with those ideas as far as the gate. Taking you by another route somewhere you aren't particular about going. All the while haranguing you for outdated citations, bullying you into a "methods overhaul," faulting you for not staying on top of something or other—after all the free seminars in equilibristics! Conferences seem dead-set on doing away with tired institutional rules like sitting still, encouraging walking out. Consider the call for *One Foot after Another*: contributions in thoughtful peregrination, mobile cerebration, walking off old-school habits, going beyond silly conventions, stepping off the well-trodden path. Or take the lecture series on the Philosophy of Running; has it a finish line? What a question! Colloquia accommodate interests from the most edified down to the most mind-boggling. Say, *Intentionalism of Restless Legs. Gentle Highwaymen and the Penny Dreadful. Holocaust Practices in Biological Perspective: The Evolution of Disgust from Pathogen Avoidance to Social Pathology.* "*The Little Engine That Could*": *A Toy-Train Model of Dopamine Reuptake. The Thermodynamics of Shoe Shuffling.*

If I eschew such gatherings and haven't attended one in ages (a fact), but nonetheless compulsively keep track of them, it is because I discovered in good time that one can occasionally use their promises as fuel for serious work or a good laugh. One starts at both ends of the candle and works towards the middle, again working through the ABCs of writing, even as one tries (fails) to raise language to a higher power, for there is as much joy and agitation in learning to write as there is in re-learning it.

Fearn Wren

(01.13.08)

I decided to leave school at noon. I had gotten it in my head that I would be more productive—*far more productive and serious*—if only I could study things by myself, without anyone trying to drum into my head redundant facts or ways of looking at the world (to see it for what it really isn't). I wanted none of that lecturing and hectoring and detaining, and when I entered this place, with the recess-end bell still ringing in the distance, I knew that I had come to the right place, had made the right decision. It was the end of winter and, with the stove ablaze in one corner and clouds of smoke rising towards the ceiling, the place looked like a steamy bathhouse, or Hell's vestibule.

I sat down on the empty chair beside a window, but when a man motioned to me to join him at his table, I moved. See all this smoke here—he asked me, looking up—and the air out there—he pointed to the windows. I think it's incredible. They are apart, but what separates them? A thin pane of glass. When all of a sudden someone opens a window—and he got up to do just that—all these foul tongues of smoke, they start licking the clean air outside, tumbling through it like dragons woken from slumber. That's what I like about this place—it makes you realize a difference like that. Same thing with the temperature. You can't see this beauty, but you can feel it. You sit in a cocoon of warmth—he continued—when suddenly, owing to a draught, a puff of cold air nips your face. And that feels heavenly. The warmth and the cold together kissing your skin. Anyhow . . . playing hooky? No—I replied. So what are you doing here? I'm going to write a film. Ever seen a film on paper? Most films look better on paper. So what's this film about? Men and gods, the crisis of faith. No kidding—then you've got your work cut out for you. And without another word he rose and went to settle with the barmaid.

Overheard that afternoon: *Ten full cartons, factory-sealed? Sure, I'll take 'em off your hands . . . Hey, no hanky-panky. Quit while you're ahead, Charek . . . Hahahaha! There's no consensus at this table. If it's consensus you want I suggest, comrade, you move over there . . . To drink or not to drink, is the question! I put it to my drinking buddies, but the mirror answers one thing, the flies another. You I don't ask, I already know where you stand . . . You're not in a rush anywhere, are you? Miss Bozhenko, how about another round for us! . . . What with my dislocated shoulder, I tell you, like a beast of burden . . . Cheer up, Honorata, you're too hard on yourself . . . I should have given him a piece of my mind, the louse! Why do I let him push me around like that? . . . No need to get worked up about it* now *when you can do it later . . . Take it from me, you're in no shape to . . . Pull yourself together. Where there's a will, there's a . . . Four-year-old boy recovering from heart surgery, but predictions are meager . . . Leukemia, the little angel, and doctors were certain she would pull through . . . What'd you call it—what's the word, what's that* word? *. . . Everyone imagines the devil with a pointed chin and pointy beard to boot—not a moustache but a beard is the sign of malefaction—but me, I always imagine the devil as having a broad chin cleft in two, like a hoof or a cunt, and his long red tongue is lured to this playground below it. That seems to me a truer image of the devil's countenance. Say, Stefan, do you figure the devil is a broad after all? No question, mate—and I'm married to her!*

The *Café-Bar Favory* was an all-time favorite dive between Paris Commune Square and the Square of the Invalids. You could always count on whiling away the hours with the *industrial Proletariat* or the *Lumpenproletariat*; if the first group was tied up manning the factories just down the Vistula, then representatives of the other group, streaming in at all hours of the day, kept you company alright. Not that they were interchangeable, the two groups. The first (according to the second) was spineless and materialistic; the second (according to the first) was mendacious and good-for-nothing. Somehow this shabby café had a conciliatory effect on everybody; one would hear of brawls and knives being pulled at the Café-Restaurant Mercury, but at the Café-Bar Favory lethargy and comity were always the order of the day. At most, from time to time someone would get the itch to show off their boxing skills. What's a broken nose? (Sad to think how Favory went under: boarded up after several years as a money-laundering beauty parlor.)

The next day I drifted around the neighborhood, feeding pigeons along train tracks and smoking near the citadel, where I chanced upon my friend Vitold, and first we went to Vitold's house on Blind Alley Street—a house one only *passed through* on account of its many entrances and exits. Come fall, its most frequent guest swept through the open doors and windows, having one year, the story goes, wantonly carried off his mother. To his blind father this was no great loss; the wind's caress, the sun's warmth, the drip of melting icicles, the song and stir of birds from the kitchen more than made up for it. To Vitold it meant misery: slovenliness, hunger, exposure to the elements, abuttal of prospects on a wall of unkempt ivy, which only drugs could clear.

Slipping out unnoticed, we quit the impasse sober. From there we went to the Café Favory. We played a game of pool, Vitold left, and I stayed until dinnertime writing a first draft of the first act of my film for an 8mm camera. On my way out, the man from the day before, whom I did not recognize sitting with his buddies, called out to me: What's happening, Ambassador? Ambassador of what?—I yelled back. The Republic of Dunces, is what! They were in stitches, and even I couldn't help laughing.

That afternoon I managed to get down some very fine ideas and some darn felicitous phrases, but I did not manage to get down the pea soup and the meatloaf. So I sat hungry, drank coffee, and didn't bother about bumming cigarettes when I could inhale the air instead. Some paunchy patrons ordered food not to drink on an empty stomach. Most attained weightlessness without it. Fundamentally, the café was only a notch above a booze can (though one could ponder their differences all day long). Spring was coming, and the evening was warmer than usual. At nightfall, a waitress tenderly pulled rubicund drapes over the scene. From the outside, the café shone like a beacon.

I began avoiding happy hour, guessing the best time to make progress on my film was early in the day. I would absent myself from the first two hours of school to watch the morning sun through the row of windows in the half-empty Bar Favory. Dust swirled, the soot-stained walls looked marmoreal, and even the culinary virtues of the place became perceptible. With crocuses and anemones on the table, I gave thought to the second act of my film.

It took place in a dilapidated church. A priest is sitting in a pew near the altar. Enter pagan gods in purple togas, with name tags and cameras dangling from their necks: Minerva, wearing strong makeup, her brow furrowed, Dionysus, evidently inebriated, and a beaming Apollo, their lips daubed with crimson. They are exploring, snapping photographs of the inner ruin soiled with pigeon droppings and lit through broken stained-glass windows (the flash goes off and a shutter clicks every few seconds). The camera follows them for a while before panning to the cassocked priest who, with eyes fixated on the floor, sidles unawares to the party of tourists. He finally takes notice of them when he finds what he is looking for beside Dionysus's sandal. Dionysus also sees the object—a walnut still in its shell—and puts his foot over it. The priest's face strains for a smile, he looks up at the god pleadingly. Dionysus brings his foot down on the nut, cracking it, and fills the church with his laughter. The priest, taken aback at first, also relaxes and begins to laugh. He is evidently happy. He is looking at the kernel, resting intact in the palm of his hand.

The Old Zholibozh heroes' brigade in gaping shirts: here they come again. Out-and-out louche types (swindlers, pickpockets, bootleggers) alongside affable boozers (bus drivers, cabmen, or porters "by day"). One of them leans his crutches against the wall and orders a cognac. In one version of this scene, he keeps to himself, doesn't say anything. The others are playing rummy. They say *table-be-set!* and the comestibles arrive; the libations commence. He sits quietly. He could be thinking anything, but his expression is wistful. They order more vodka, he orders another cognac. Someone asks: don't you want to play rummy with us? Not today—he answers— I'm not in the mood. Be sure to tell us when you are. I'm not in the mood, that's all. You've been saying that since your accident. More morose every day, this guy. How can anyone help you if you won't let yourself be helped? If I can't help myself no-one can. Good day—he says, grabbing his crutches. See you same time tomorrow . . . But the next day he doesn't show. No-one knows where he is. He's probably gone—vouches one of them—to the Sisters Adorers of the Blood of Christ to ask them to pray for him. They give no guarantees.

How long did I hang about there, listening in and watching, as an outsider? I had a penchant for fraternizing with the disenfranchised, whose disenfranchisement was written into the overall scheme of things political and could in no way be erased. When one interloped as I did, sitting apart and bent on recording that unfilmable film, taking up space for hours on end, one was at the mercy of the "kings" and "queens," the regular clientele and waitressing distaff, their hair dyed purple with gentian. One moment *persona non grata*, the next drinking *Bruderschaft*. One could not avoid being treated badly, taunted, bemused, or amused.

The symbolism of a walnut is ponderous and potentially unintelligible (no need to be ashamed of such symbolism if one writes a film never meant to get off the page). I give the priest a long monologue to recite, a bit artificial and elevated, plenty rhymed, but absolutely dramatically indispensable. There goes Vitold again, leading his father from the doctor.

Once more I'd like to ask you, o Lord,
Not to absolve but to hear me out.
I stare into your azure-blue orb,
But, forgive me, you cannot have me.
Keep your judgment, I know you are cross with me;
You, the essence of anger, let the herd obey you.
What dulcified my conscience, o Lord,
What gave shape to and stiffened my resolve,
What wanted to light up like a star beside you—
I once owned myself, in my youth,
Robbed anon, cast into every form of bondage,
I came here for shelter and to worship you,
But was subjected to baptism, communions,
A new name, and these vows.
I began plotting my escape
And carried around a token of it,
To give me courage, to comfort me;
And I lost it when, one day,
It rolled from my hand.
For years I have not overlooked a spot,
As a mouse I poked around every hole,
Yet am certain it is here somewhere;
Just let me look again.
Here I search for my happiness,
Year after year I cross this threshold,
With frantic hope and false dithering,
And indifference swallows my heart when I leave.

The film began in an apartment high-rise. The camera operator was to take a freight elevator from the top floor all the way down, filming glimpses of each storey through the window in the elevator door. He would recite a prologue, something of a moral parable. The prologue would end as the elevator stops in a pitch-black basement. The operator then opens the door, switches on the light in the main corridor, and proceeds into the depths of the basement. He turns right into a narrow passage, turns left. It is a maze, this basement, with cellars just like prison cells. He walks on, turning lights on as he goes. A flickering draws him into a short passage where someone had lit a candle. Through slits in the door to one of the cellars he sees a wide-eyed man. He is weeping on his hands and knees.

In an alternative version of this scene, the camera would be lowered on a rope from my balcony like a sausage. Balconies are typically lousy with junk, famished dogs, and pigeons' nests, while cellars

are impenetrably murky, dank and noxious; each has its advantages. The man whom the cameraman encounters would be sitting on the last (first-floor) balcony, holding on to the bars of the railing. He would be in a similar state of distraction, his speech slurred, casting his glance wildly about him. It could be he wants to do away with himself, to dissolve into everything, but is afraid. The two men—the dissembling priest and this wild-eyed prisoner—were meant to be "as one." They were the same psyche groping for opposing solutions to the same dilemma.

Who can tell whether I was

casting these lost souls as lunatics, or these lunatics as lost souls—they seemed mad and frail when they were simply lost like all of us, indistinguishable from the rest. Their confusion about God—the *highest confusion*—was the condition of their psychic malady. Their need for faith was bound up with episodes of lunacy. The twilight of faith was limited (as it should be) to doubts about right and wrong, about how to live without sin, to keep on an even keel. They were plunged into moral darkness by their over-reliance on reason, was how I saw it, and lowly reason was the cornerstone of faith. I still see a kernel of truth in this simple, unstated conclusion. Forget the sun—he said to me—it is slaughter, it is a hangman and we are all dangling from his noose, it is our putrefying flesh. Life—he says—is darkness.

Fearn Wren

(01.24.08)

It is an awful satire, and an epigram on the materialism of our modern age, that nowadays the only use that can be made of solitude is imposing it as a penalty, as jail. What difference there is between those times when, no matter how secular materialism always was, man believed in the solitude of the convent, when, in other words, solitude was revered as the highest, as the destiny of Eternity—and the present when it is detested as a curse and is used only for the punishment of criminals. Alas, what a change. (Søren Kierkegaard)

Indeed, modern secular culture regards solitude as either a form of punishment or an insignia of mental illness. It has largely lost faith in solitude as a spiritual experience, let alone as a lifestyle choice. If the modern state uses discipline and isolation in corrections, it is in part because the combination proved morally effective in religious training. The church may have made the original investment in discipline and solitude, but the state claims most of the dividends. For centuries now it disciplines the individual with punitive and pedagogical means—it passes him through a meat grinder and expects his re-form. For his soul it cares not.

It was thanks to multiple forms of secular regimentation that *self-discipline* shed its spiritual meaning of integrity in the face of odds, quandaries, and disasters, and acquired another: efficacy. As for solitude, it is nowadays usually sought not as an end in itself (moral or spiritual end) but as a means to fulfilling practical obligations when all else has failed. There are still people who sequester themselves seeking a simpler life, or woodsmen who withdraw for periods into the wilderness, drawn to a wilderness solitude, or those who flirt for a time with asceticism or monasticism—but they are, needless to say, notable exceptions. Such amateurs of the solitary life run the risk, greater than ever before, of becoming the outcasts and pariahs of society. When isolation cannot be productive, when it cannot be

milked in one's dealings with others, then it is an insufferable imposition, whose benefits are never recognized in time, or not at all.
This "fruitless" imposition of solitude, be it prescribed or accidental, is viewed invariably as punishment, meted out by adverse circumstances, the malice of fate, or institutions enforcing this-worldly
justice and order. The school and prison systems pretend, of course,
to much more than mere punishment—or to much less: to break
behavior, to correct flaws, if not in a person's character, then at least
in their conduct, for life. To be sure, the educational system makes
formative claims where the prison system makes *reformative* ones, but
at the very core, the educational system is carceral and the carceral
system educational. In both the *factorial* principle is entrenched: on
one level, subjects undergo assembly-line transformation, on another
level, their unpaid or low-paid labor fuels an industry. In schools that
labor is called *intellectual* even when it consists of mindless regurgita-
tion; in prisons it is overwhelmingly *manual*, relieving one monot-
ony with another. Behind their closed doors, of course, they are still
sharing blueprints.

Kneel and you shall believe. Kneel and you shall be drunk on words.

People are right to give the tightest possible barriers to the human mind. In study, as in everything else, its steps must be counted and regulated for it. (Montaigne)

Even the prison yard, around which one is at liberty to pace, or the school yard, where one is free to break one's legs, are merely analogues of one's cell or school bench. The periodically extended disciplinary release from study and solitude forever distorts the ethics of both (study and solitude).

Dangerous offenders turn themselves in or are removed from society, after which they are tried, convicted, and put away. Regardless of the official policy of protecting societal norms, they are restrained from losing themselves further in the spiral of society, which manipulates, exploits, and imprisons as insidiously and indiscriminately—in a word, as *criminally*—as does a prison. With basic needs (food and shelter) provided for, they are given time to be alone with themselves so as to get along better with others. For every one behind bars there are two running free.

At Genoa, the word Liberty *may be read over the front of the prisons and on the chains of the galley-slaves. This application of the device is good and just. It is indeed only malefactors of all estates who prevent the citizen from being free. In the country in which all such men were in the galleys, the most perfect liberty would be enjoyed. (Jean-Jacques Rousseau, less-than-model Citizen of Geneva, periodic recluse)*

It can be argued that through imprisonment isolation can finally convert itself into spiritual nourishment. The prisoner is given time to reflect on his past and the here and now; perhaps he is given inspirational literature to read and is inspired; perhaps he only re-reads scripture out of boredom, but is intrigued by passages on suffering and sin. He is now, as it were, outside the world and this enables him to consider his place in the world more objectively. Without going to any great length—through introspection—he may eventually emancipate himself from the prison of self-ignorance, be rehabilitated as a citizen, and rewarded with a state of grace.

Hermitages do not make hermits . . . prisons do not make prisoners. (Don W. Kleine, academic, in reference to Thoreau)

The rare prisoner who reconciles himself to being punished—judging his conviction rightful and the punishment meted out to him merciful or parsimonious—who makes peace with himself and actually passes his time in solitary contemplation—he could well leave the prison (if he leaves it) half punished and half a better man. He'd have a prison to thank for it. Prison had given him an opportunity to mend his ways and organized his life for him. He might have chosen to throw this opportunity away by taking his life—to act against the prison and its rules, to reject this morally regenerative (morally regressive) system, to wrest his ultimate freedom from the arms of penal authority. That freedom, the *full extent* of his freedom, was suspended after he abused it; in being thrown in jail and subjected to its correctional routine, he was deprived of a sense of autonomy. He was permitted to drink his fill only of discipline and solitude. Is it so surprising, then, that he should take advantage of the latter and seek refuge within himself from his outward incapacitation?

[A] population undergoing drastic change is a population of misfits, and misfits live and breathe in an atmosphere of passion. There is a close connection between lack of confidence and the passionate state of mind and . . . passionate intensity can serve as a substitute for confidence. (Eric Hoffer, migratory worker, solitary)

And the wretchedness of those free to fall through the cracks? I used to be part of a society undergoing radical change. Not anymore; the society I now live in enjoys a good measure of stability and control, unlike the society I lived in before, a *transitional* and in many ways *lawless* society, with misfits from all walks of life. All the addictions and violence assuaging (abetting) their wretchedness—poor confidence-substitutes they must have been. Their prolonged, collective, dynamic "state of passion" wasn't the reliable kind the thinker had in mind. It ruined people I knew; one by one, they dropped like flies after a passionate (pathetic) struggle with the windowpane. Perhaps this was because we were all sinners, idlers without ambition, mettle, or moral fiber. Most of all, we lacked discipline. Life was a pleasurable daze and our intentions slippery; everyone, absolutely everyone could be bribed and everything, absolutely everything could be circumvented. We'd make a mockery of the law and "get away with murder." A demon at our back egged us on, telling us things were dandy.

The primary and most beautiful of Nature's qualities is motion, which agitates her at all times, but this motion is simply a perpetual consequence of crimes, she conserves it by means of crimes only; the person who most nearly resembles her, and therefore the most perfect being, necessarily will be the one whose most active agitation will become the cause of many crimes . . . (Donatien-Alphonse-François de Sade, passionate inmate of prisons and asylums)

This philosophy, like all philosophies, surely had personal grounds, was the rationalization of personal excess. The matter is open to speculation. Did the libertine first commit crimes to give wings to the writer, to deprave with pen alone? Not to work crimes into books, but to work books into crimes in periods of release. Including new book-crimes (unacknowledged bastards some). A signature body of work, signature crimes. Sealing his freedom to write by way of isolation, to commit new crimes to paper from the *carceri*. Perverting prison discipline into games of arousal. Some claim the Marquis suffered from graphomania, a nervous condition, making his desire for solitude all the more exigent—more of a compulsion really. I say he got off having his way with language. When authorities caught on, they took away his tools; with bare hands only he could do nothing.

Passionate sinning has not infrequently been an apprenticeship to sainthood. (Hoffer)

In advocating the benefits of imprisonment, I am of course speaking of the ideal prison, the just sentence, the model prisoner. I do believe criminals should be given a push towards solitude; it may yet liberate them when they are chained. And, as Rousseau and countless others after him maintained, society itself is a lot like a prison. The converse is also true: prisons reproduce—in a controlled and, in many respects, safer environment—the basic structure of "free" social relations: economic, political, sexual (they also reproduce the worst in those relations).

Under a government which imprisons any unjustly, the true place for a just man is also a prison. (Henry David Thoreau, prisoner for one night, recluse)

Despite being relatively free, we feel ourselves to be unfree most of the time. Our hands are bound not only by public laws and duties, but also by private affairs. Language itself has been called the prison-house of the mind, though it frees us to be solitary and helps us endure being alone. You do your writing, reading, thinking in solitude; you pass your solitude writing, reading, thinking. You say language constrains your nature, your being? Then "know thyself" in solitude. You say you feel locked in? But that is just megalomaniacal brooding. If you lack the disposition to solitude, you will not strike it in any surroundings; if you are predisposed to it, you will kindle it anywhere.

Tranquility is found also in dungeons; but is that enough to make them desirable places to live in? The Greeks imprisoned in the cave of the Cyclops lived there very tranquilly, while they were awaiting their turn to be devoured. (Rousseau)

The more you try not to sound like a devil's advocate, the more you sound like the epitome of a devil's advocate. At some point, you realize you have crossed over an invisible line to the other side, and, furthermore, that you remain convinced. This is often the fate of apodictic arguments against common sense, against "genius in its working clothes." In theory, the prison is one of the few places where submission to discipline is non-negotiable and solitude fully sanctioned. In practice, there are prisons, and there are prisons; some segregate, others congregate their inmates (different prisoners have different "needs"). Many are plagued by overcrowding. Solitude is not always to be found in them, and often it is a luxury. Prison-life is often a school of depravity, a vicious cycle of abuse. One listens to what ex-convicts are *actually saying about prison life*, and they commonly say things like: "It's a zoo in there" (even if it wasn't a zoo), or "it's a madhouse" (though no-one laid a hand upon them), or "it's a nightmare" (though it was smooth sailing), or "it's a moral cesspool" (did they keep their head above the muck?). Those in charge caution against treating such accounts at face value, citing the moral degradation of prisoners. But I know better; their words are euphemisms. The majority is corrupted by the prison; they are ceaselessly contriving ways to assert their freedom in captivity and subvert carceral discipline; they dodge solitude because it makes despair more poignant, because to them it is torture. For some a stay in prison— even a supposedly humane and reformed prison—really is a "death-trap." They go through a terrible time and go insane or do away with themselves.

S. D. *Chrostowska*

Solitude is thin as ice. It is a walk on water.
I spent several afternoons with my friend Pavel Vorman following his release from the detention centre in Bialoleka, still the largest penal complex in Europe. Soon after, Vorman was killed in a motorcycle accident and I attended my first funeral. "It was unbearable," he told me about his time in prison. He was technically a recidivist; this was his second sentence, for armed robbery; he was familiar with the conditions. "I knew what I was getting into," he confessed, "but I thought I would get away with it" (he was referring to his trial, the favorable outcome of which hung on the non-appearance of a witness). He had a jailbird tattoo which put him on a respectable rung of the criminal hierarchy: a black "swallow" in the outer corner of his eye ("At least I'm no *frajer*"). Whether in prison or out of prison, he was not what you would call a sucker. He was what you might call a walking paradox: a gentle guy with a short fuse, a decent guy who continually fell in with scoundrels. They turned to him for help, and he counted them among his *closest* friends. In spite of a history of violence, he always, and especially of late, appeared as a quiet and sensitive type. That is why I liked so much to spend time with him. I wanted to learn what happened to him, what made him seem so pacified and eager to make a clean breast of it. He seemed ready to take stock of his "dirty" actions and experiences, and I gladly lent him my ear. I was happy for him; he had come to grips with some inner demon that had previously put him at risk of evil influence. Seeing in his face the afterglow of epiphanies associated with his life, I wanted to learn from him.

Vorman's wasn't the only such prison story. There are countless accounts that partake in this internal contradiction: life inside is hell, but it is also atonement and spiritual release, and forced solitude makes all the difference. But it was Vorman who threw things into relief for me: who told me about the warm breeze entering his cell ("hardly a cell in the old-school sense"), about "watching a cactus grow," about feeling simultaneously at peace with himself and excited at the thought of finally buying a motorcycle and making amends to his mother and siblings ("fragile and impressionable" he called them, as though he were describing himself).

That spring, we met on a rotting bench in the thicket of burdock and elder behind my building (a primary school was later built on that lot). Violence was breaking out everywhere. It coursed through the air, sprouting scuffles, elbows and malisons, in store queues, cafeterias, and waiting rooms; one could not avoid catching whiff of it. Just a few months before, a son hacked his father with an axe one floor below mine—the two were having an argument, the son became enraged and went after the father, chased the father amuck up and down the corridor before dealing him a deadly blow in the back on their doorstep. The bloodstains had not yet been wiped up when I went to look at the crime scene, unable to imagine the scene of such a crime right beneath my feet, in this serene but, it now struck me, furtively somber building. And before that, I believe it was late December, a young woman was pushed out of an eleventh-storey window onto the lawn beside the apothecary shop. Starlings flocked to that spot, attracted by fresh blood. Both murders had been unpremeditated, quite the crimes of passion.

Vorman did not go on about his prison experience; I questioned him, but "between us" there were things he "would rather not talk about" (injecting chocolate into his lung so as to be sent to the infirmary was one of them). His face flushed and he remained evasive about many details; I suspect this was less because of aloofness than shame in his "moral weakness." I am reminded now that he often used the phrase "moral weakness" and emphasized that it was completely separate from "physical weakness." "I saw many morally rich cowards and strongmen who were moral bankrupts," he assured me. The scars on his arms, from what must have been self-lacerations, spoke for themselves but told a cryptic story. As for us, we would finally drop the subject of prison and move on to other things—things, as he emphatically put it, "with a future." The late-spring sun dappled our faces, animated with spinning our plans.

Fearn Wren

(02.19.08)

No matter how hard I try, I may never reconcile the disharmony between my thoughts and my actions, my intentions and my deeds. Not that I claim to be uniquely afflicted with this condition! It is all too common, I suppose; it is the rule. But I have the pleasure (the pain) of knowing only my lot and coping with it all on my own. Many tire of it—you can see they will tire of it as soon as they hear it (the disharmony), by the way they "put their finger on it" in some youthful *cri de coeur*, on the advent of their adulthood. But I may never tire of trying to rectify that essential discord.

The great philanthropist and educator Pestalozzi saw the moral and true individual as the centre of harmonious spheres. "The circle of knowledge commences close around a man, and from thence stretches out concentrically," he noted in his programmatic essay, *The Evening Hour of a Hermit* (1780). Knowledge is, above all, skill in living; to obtain it is to live more and more proficiently. "Not art, not books, but life itself is the true basis of teaching and education." The rings that bind us to society, bind us to ourselves and within ourselves, must be brought into consonance with each other.

There was a time in my life when the two—my will and my actions—were in perfect accord. I made a vow to myself and kept it. At the beginning, I liked to call it my turnaround, *my watershed*.

When I entered adolescence, the age of European wars and violent uprisings had long ended. The Balkans were at each others' throats, but the rest of Europe had suffered its share of belligerence and needed to regroup. Thinking back to the crass metamorphoses I myself would undergo in just a few short years, I read in them the unmistakable symptoms of a *revolutionary void* which needed filling, but which could not be filled with ideas and actions devoid of a meaningful cause or fellow feeling.

But precisely this limbo in which the youth of my generation found itself made *hollow actions* possible and even necessary. It emboldened one to *sound* this hollowness, to flaunt it—in a word, to squander the freedom which the older generations had secured after centuries of bondage.

Ours was a particularly thankless withdrawal from the political. Even on the level of youth movements and iconoclasm we had nothing authentic to offer. We couldn't care less for a home-grown youth culture. The stimuli to produce something authentic were plentiful: political freedom (unprecedented in the history of our parents, their parents, their parents' parents, and so on), the electric jolts of youth, exposure to the West's disenchantment with itself. That is plenty of firepower, if you ask me; it should have sufficed to bring about something culturally germane, to set off a chain reaction, a conflagration of ridiculous stereotypes and prejudices unique to this part of the world. Nothing of the sort transpired. In our brazen recklessness we carried on like soldiers of a disbanded army.

The vacuity of our resistance—in second-hand forms and without a progressive purpose—may ultimately be to blame for my generation's gross psycho-social retardation. It may also lie behind my failure to remember those years in all but the vaguest outline. It would seem that only those who carried themselves like visitors on the socio-political margins (rather than being their full-fledged members), who had about them a barely perceptible air of detachment (non-participation), and who (when one probed them) had a great view but a hazy grasp of the pseudo-anarchistic circus—only these *observers*, it would seem, evaded its degenerative process. Could it be that this sidelines' vision brought with it an *uncommitted memory*—that, in other words, one had to resign oneself to an essential blank in one's biography, a run of "lost years"?

It must be because of this thoroughly *unnatural* course of events—an entire generation's potential going to seed—that I set off on my wild-goose chase. I should mention here another happy convergence: a truly one-in-a-lifetime convergence between parent and child. For once, our talks did not founder, but were brought to a mutually respectful resolution. I would be leaving. I would at long last be leaving that forsaken and unsightly city, which instead of becoming prettier became uglier by the day. I warrant that by now it is Europe's ugliest capital—I have just seen it with my own eyes, as I have seen several other capitals, and without a doubt it is (or is fast becoming). In Warsaw, with Soviet-style architecture replacing many post-war ruins, things could only go from bad to worse. The most recent construction boom, geared to catching up to the West, was articulated in hypermodern simulacra that shot skyward beside slighted historical monuments. Even the latter were suspect, I realized. Even the cobblestones. As a resident of this city, I had moved through a large-scale reconstruction (the Old Town); I had gone about my life in a counterfeit landscape, rebuilt from the ground up and passed off as authentic. Though much of this rebuilding was done before my time, nobody put up plaques commemorating the reconstruction; they only put up plaques commemorating the *original construction* of buildings no longer in existence. A reconstruction to erase the destruction. An illusion to make good the memory of loss. An oversight and an obfuscation. Of course, one passed by the Royal Castle or what remained of it and saw the cranes, the trucks spinning concrete, the people from the restoration commission overseeing the rise of this sham Phoenix from ashes and dust. But one turned a blind eye; so irresistible was the illusion one could not help falling for it. The *historical* Royal Castle rose again—that is to say, a replica of the original architectural work of art rose in its stead—yet *here was the Royal Castle, the very same.* Meanwhile, rubble which should have been cleared before all else lay as before. With each passing year, it becomes clearer just how much *moral rubble* was left.

I cannot help thinking of my departure from Warsaw and from Poland as an *evacuation*—so great was my urgency and relief when at last I had left. But there was also sadness about going. Sadness coupled with helplessness. I was quitting a great many things I sensed would soon vanish and I would not see them through to their vanishing point. By dint of my escape, their value would be magnified a hundredfold. Harking back to those things—so many and so disparate—was sure to become a source of internal turmoil when least expected. The pangs of voluntary and involuntary exile are painted with the same brush.

The new chapter began when I fell upon the idea of studying overseas as a solution to all my problems: my Polish predicament, my Polish derailment, my Polish obscurity. I had drifted awfully close to the vortex of my environment; it was the last chance to extricate myself from its pull. I had gone to secondary school in an erstwhile military complex; shooting targets still graced the interior of its concrete enclosure. During its short lifespan, it was one of the laxest schools imaginable, which had to do as much with the novelty of a charter school run by a breakaway collective as with its patron saint, the famed author of *Ferdydurke*, satirist of overweening conservatism, pedantry, and rote learning. Only the most progressive could set their children loose in this menagerie, which had no library to speak of and hardly any books. At the graduation ceremony, a great bard furiously strummed his acoustic, mesmerizing us with political songs.

No more Polish schooling, I said to myself; from now on only American schooling. *My American education*—the various anachronistic and sentimental notions I had of it, the sentimentalism that very phrase evoked—the kind of education I would have versus the kind I (for the life of me) would not have, the consummate education for a late bloomer, which would transform an overwrought personality into a grounded one and a poorly tuned musing organ into a finely tuned thinking machine. I did not *entertain* for long the possibility of going away; I made up my mind to leave at once, under the pretext of being incapable of studying or of pursuing a career in a formalistic backwater—this was a *sense* I had, but I put it across as a passionate *conviction*. (Either way one is shunted from one prison to another, one's choices limited to manacles or chain-gang.)

Were I to trace back to its source my need to leave this place, I would probably put down the bulk of it to the view from my window. With such a view greeting you on overcast mornings and at suppertime, you succumbed to either a stupor-solitude or existential doom—the feeling of being on the edge of the world and about to fall off. In the autumn, by virtue of its location—the thirteenth storey on the northernmost point of a vast housing complex—volleys of crows blackened the sky just outside with a deafening collective screech. Stranded above a dismal arboreal expanse, I often coped by casting my mind beyond that forest to a cluster of peculiarly named streets—*Museum, Alphabet, Hieroglyph, Papyri, Metaphor,* and *Prose*—which I recollected through the haze of childhood (having once pedaled through them with my father). And by this habit of casting my mind further and further outward, I eventually cast myself to a new world.

At one juncture in this journey away from Poland and towards America (a journey of periodic returns to my country and growing estrangement from it), I committed a theft, bringing upon myself the state and its laws. I was found with a library book stuffed in the small of my back. My decision to steal may have been impulsive, acting on it required only a moment's sobriety, but my intention was clear. Only I was unclear about my intention. I do not exaggerate, for instance, when I say that I *let* myself be apprehended. I remember my transports at having been "booked," my giddy laughter at being "dragged down to earth" by my crime. In Poland I had made off with scores of books without getting caught; but, had I been, no one would have cared. But here they took even the most *petit theft* as a grave offence against the state, punished you with heavy fines and manual labor. Of course, had the judge taken into consideration the book itself, whose title alone (*The Existential Imagination*) spoke volumes about its thief, he could have deduced that I used crime to gain insight into the ruthlessness—the absurd ruthlessness—of a functional legal and penal apparatus. Until that point, as a Pole I knew only slipshod bureaucracy, slovenly law enforcement, venal justice. Had the judge only considered the title of that book (better yet, its contents) he would have known that the best punishment for me was a pardon. And if he considered also the circumstances of the misdemeanor, his inference would have been doubly confirmed. But he did not consider the book any more than the context. And the context was this: an arsonist at large, meticulously setting fire to university buildings, one after another, perversely, several days in a row. Which is to say: I perpetrated my crime under the influence of an exceptional set of circumstances. These exceptional circumstances in my case amounted to extenuating circumstances. I committed a small crime just as another, far greater crime was being committed. It would be perfectly fair to say that in committing my crime I came under the influence of that other crime. With so many police patrolling the university—particularly its libraries—I was aroused to commit a petty crime of my own. I committed the crime simply because I could not abide the suspense of this manhunt. The hunting of one individual put everyone else on the edge of their seats. The way those blue men and women hunted for the arsonist made you wish you were hunted yourself. Their dogged focus alone made you want to commit a misdeed out in the open, right under their noses. Not because you were convinced they would pay no mind to you, not out of contempt for police duty, but to test their watchfulness, their readiness for duty. And perhaps by distracting them to help the other get away, to share in his guilt, face a little prosecution, feel a little *mens rea* yourself. Had the judge considered these extenuating circumstances, he would have exonerated me.

The punishment did not end in the courthouse. The university had its own disciplinary code and penalties. Mine was a supernumerary assignment, in keeping with its mission of mental labor. What they wanted from me was a statement of guilt and contrition. What they got instead was a statement of defense, an *apologia* flying in the face of my punishment. The counselor reviewing it, the irony obviously lost on him, did not frown upon my arguments, not even the most preposterous of them. I was adamant, for example, that in Poland book-theft was not a punishable offence. That it was *customary* in Poland to swipe books from libraries, because most good books were out-of-print and in demand and would inevitably be stolen. Even my aunt (I amazed myself by actually invoking my aunt's authority to build up my argument), a retired school librarian with over thirty-five years of experience, was lenient on the issue of book theft. Whenever she lent out books from her personal collection, I maintained, she did not expect them to be returned ("I will always find other books to close the gaps!"). Such partings did not determine which books she allowed one to borrow. "The changing of hands by books is the greatest joy for a dedicated librarian—for whom being a librarian is not a chore but a *life calling*." "Only librarians ill-suited to the job would be bothered by the free comings and goings of books." "An indefinite loan isn't theft." And "Books circulate."

Some years needed to pass before I went on the payroll of a university police department. I patrolled school buildings with a flashlight and shortwave radio on the lookout for suspicious persons and security hazards. Among my ancillary duties was dropping off human eyeballs at the macabre "Eye Bank," in a container tagged "Sandman, PhD." In the years in which I scoured the university premises at night, half the time was spent exploring. I carried, so to speak, two pairs of eyes: one for performing my duties, the other for sating my curiosity. The night patrol broadened greatly my knowledge of the university. Places which by day were congenial to me appeared menacing in the sulphuric light. And vice versa: those I thought unhomely before nightfall I gravitated to after dark. Surprising resemblances often presented themselves to the eye between objects that by day were as unlike each other as could be. One realized that the dispossessed were also residents (and onetime students) of the university. One found them asleep in basements and libraries. A homicide would be committed, and one would witness the removal of a corpse—as happened with one *cadaver-handler*, in the morgue of the university's Gross Anatomy Department, whose murderer and co-worker (co-handler of corpses) burned down his parish church and set ablaze two others, then took his own life in Bluffers Park that same night.

(Lurid details these; but every revenge homicide has its lurid details.) As I thus got to know the university after dark and after hours, I also learned more about the university (and at the university). One could say that all my hands-on extracurricular activities within the

136

university—including invigilation and usherdom—were learning activities, not unlike academics, though subordinate to academics. All of them were designed to bring you back safely to your studies, not take you away from them.

At another juncture in my university education, I was putting on Hamlet. I wanted to stage Hamlet the play as well as play Hamlet the man. My abbreviated version of the tragedy revolved around Hamlet's indecisiveness, the discrepancy between his thoughts and his actions—its most dramatically challenging aspect. All the pieces, as they say, fell into place: the funds, the crew, the actors, and a stage to upstage the great hall at Elsinore. I walked around the college for weeks memorizing monologues, I learned fencing to know how to handle a foil, I strongly identified with the protagonist, yet, after much wavering, I could not bring myself to act the part. My ineptitude as an actor of Hamlet could not but put into question my aptitude as a director of *Hamlet*. This irresponsibility, thinly disguised as responsibility, threw a wrench into the gears of my play. At the last minute a new Hamlet had to be found and, suddenly, the other pieces fell out of place—the funds proved insufficient, the stage-hall was re-booked for other events, and the crew, at loggerheads. And so, the superb idea of staging *Hamlet* (of staging none other than *Hamlet!*) fell through; but that, of all plays, *Hamlet* should fall through seemed strangely apropos. I used to regret this miscarried performance and play, but my view of it changed in the recounting. As it seems to me now, in my vacillation to play Hamlet, I may have succeeded at playing him after all.

Not long after this fiasco, which set me behind in my studies while also being part of my studies, it dawned on me that surviving my so-called Liberal Arts education required little more than going through the motions of learning in lockstep. Sticking one's neck out for Shakespeare (or anything else for that matter) was a mistake. Further along in one's university career, with the safeguards gone, one could disengage from the chain. Things would not be laid out as neatly as before and, left to one's own devices, one would learn to cut corners—but that's the flip side of liberty. Pestalozzi was an incurable idealist. Even the following tenet of "Pestalozzianism"—whose best principles and methods were allegedly implemented in American schools, banishing rote learning and corporal punishment—was a pragmatist's pipe dream, bound to clash with capitalism and individualism:

> Education is nothing more than the polishing of each single link in the great chain that binds humanity together and gives it unity. The failings of education and human conduct spring as a rule from our disengaging a single link and giving it special treatment as though it were a unit in itself, rather than a part of a chain. It is as though we thought the strength and utility of the link came from its being silver-plated, gilded, or even jeweled, rather than from its being joined unweakened to the links next to it, strong and supple enough to share with them the daily stresses and strains of the chain. (Pestalozzi, *The Education of Man*)

In the American university, I had found not a way out but a hideout. I disappeared, forgot, and was forgotten. Part of this forgetting was afforded by intensively living and thinking in another language, by escaping into that language. And writing in this foreign idiom from the start as if it were my own, my native language—from the start taking liberties with it, commanding it, bending its rules with half-formed ideas. If Polish was my mother tongue, English was my father tongue; if Polish was my maiden language, English was the language I betrothed. Both equally gremial and equally strange. Little did I know that English, a stubborn language, instead of blossoming in my hands, would yield only a clipped, stilted, wooden diction—the purview of academic literature. Nothing so demonstrates the detrimental effects of Anglo-Saxon education on a Polish intelligence—an education which mangles your writing at every stage (like linen is mangled, so all the creases in one's prose, which make it engaging, are flattened out)—nothing demonstrates these effects better than the present state of my prose. Several persons have remarked, on the one hand, the abstract and austere ("Teutonic"!) style of some of my unpublished stories, and, on the other, the metaphorical ("Slavic"!) prolixity I often resort to in my published essays. But the dullness of my communication, which, try as I might, I cannot completely conceal from you, is the effect of letting *standard academic English* have its way with me. The restiveness you read in these pages is in fact an allergic reaction to the standard prose style disseminated throughout American academe. Judging by the labored awkwardness of this note and by how long it has taken me to convey what needed to be conveyed concerning my vita until this time last year, the subject itself—"my American education," "my existence in English"—must be especially disagreeable to me.

But new ideas! Crackling new ideas—assumed, identified with, as good as my own—were everywhere. Whenever I think of ideas in general, I always fall back on figuration:

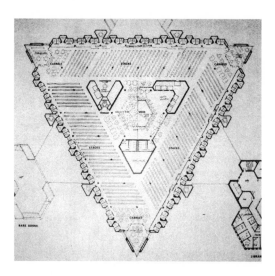

A triangle-based monolith—the central library, the library of libraries, the library of sub-libraries, a veritable *mise en abyme*. Its shelves bulging with intellectual inventory, much of it waiting to be dusted off and rediscovered. And if the ideas bodied forth in them became negligible—a rarity to be sure, as all such expired ideas have a *fateful* appeal, holding out the promise of life-altering adventures—then at least the dust trapped inside these volumes, the powder shed by their disintegrating covers could be harvested and snuffed in small doses. As I got older—twelve years was long enough to grow old—I liked nothing more than this diving for ideas that have not surfaced in a very long time. There are whole oceans of ideas looming in the depths of university libraries that may never again see the light of day.

Ideas that held particular sway over my mind arranged themselves memorably in my imagination. The more fanciful and inordinate of such conceits took on the poses of topiaries, separated by the hedges of heteroclite categories; others, for modesty, took to creeping and rambling, protecting their entanglements with muscular tendrils and foliage. Many of these recondite, chimerical "specimens" fell from the lips of old professors who, ex cathedra, tricked me into thinking they were relevant—those antiquated ideas of theirs—even *supremely* relevant. As they spouted their ideas, they grew in my eyes to the size of intellectual giants. But overtop their musical phrasing one *heard* scratches—as I did when I last listened to tape recordings of their lectures—and one *saw* through cracks in their veneer their very irrelevance. One remembers their dirty fingernails, their lopsided shoes, the rubber bands around their earpieces, and one knows them for who they really were.

But my awakening to the benefits of learning antedated all that. I can pinpoint the exact circumstances of this adolescent awakening: an essay—as far as I am concerned, the only worthwhile essay I have ever composed—on the topic of ugliness in literature. For the first time, I became wholly engrossed in an idea—the idea of ugliness; not in any concrete and actual ugliness, but in the depiction of ugliness, not in painting but literature. I pored over my schoolbooks, aching to put everything I ever wanted to learn and say about ugliness and its perennial struggle with beauty into my essay, completely intoxi-cated with the nervous secretions of ratiocination. It does not take much to enfeeble the body. With the mind it is different. The mind remains elastic and clear on most days; some evenings a dark cloud hangs over it, the weariness of repetition, the heaviness of anxiety. But on most days, it is the sun that defines its gradual unhurried trajectory, the waxing and waning of reason. Only when the mind is hit by obsession or derangement will you see it reel. It forges ahead clearing everything in its path or stumbling over it until, limp, it is delivered from its travail. That essay was a case in point. My teacher, used to receiving from me only sloppy work of mediocre quality, facetiously drawled that I had written a book. It was for me the dawn of Sisyphean labor of mind.

My idea of pursuing this labor wherever it would lead was born around that time. Which brings me back to the mighty conjunc-tion of will and action with which I began. Such a perfect conjunc-tion can seem a blessing—and it was indeed—but more often it is a double-edged sword. "Perhaps the most fateful gift an evil genius could bestow upon our times is knowledge without skill" (Pesta-lozzi). Once you have tasted the pleasures of knowledge, you are in it for the long haul. You find it hard to resist. Like a skier on the brow of a hill, propelled by the hill's very incline, you let your runners carry you wherever they please. That blinding slope is not a disaster waiting to happen, but a destiny already happening. You fulfill this destiny willy-nilly, let come what may.

For twelve years I saw nothing beyond this destiny: I saw no way out of America with its universities. Some would say, sarcastically, that for twelve years I was not at work but on holiday, not work-ing hard but vacationing hard. But the truth is I heard the crack of a whip and I heeded it. The mystique of discipline sent me into ecstasy. For certain individuals—let's say "problem individuals"—the structure of higher education is a godsend. Their intellectual poten-tial cannot develop in any other setting. I was one of them. I threw myself into my studies with single-minded fervor.

If there are words that best describe my old university, they would be *an oasis*. It existed at the heart of a metropolis as an island amid civic and suburban drabness. One confined oneself within its walls like a voluntary prisoner. If, four years on, one still had no conception of the shape of the greater city, it was due to its insular character. On the other hand, one knew the shape of this oasis like the back of one's hand. One knew it by day, one knew it by night; one knew it at all hours and in all states of consciousness. One had one's own map of it, drawn with one's own mind: there were darkened buildings one had entirely to oneself, but which by day one did not recognize; some sites were breached under duress, others entered only out of compulsion; from one year to the next certain places would become off-limits, simply cease to exist on one's private map. Certain no-trespass zones marked off the past from the present. The university formed a society unto itself. Its paternal provosts, maternal caretakers (mostly Polish), and avuncular night porters (mostly Irish) were a grotesque familial body. Of course, its appeal for me never turned on its classes and sense of community, but on its reading rooms and sense of isolation.

When you entered such a university, you saw only a forest, were overwhelmed and instantly became lost in this forest. It was hard to make out individual trees in that agglomerate of trees. Then, one day, the scales fell from your eyes; what you saw was no forest at all, but just one tree, a colossal oak-tree. And that you were a graft on this tree and would grow in tandem with it through the ages. Whenever you were out of your element, moving in the world outside the university, you saw only scrawny, isolated trees; their sylvan cohesion remained invisible. And you felt like you had been felled.

On most days you left the house only for brief periods. You rarely socialized with more than one person at a time. You grew rusty at socializing. At a lecture entitled (o horror of horrors) "The Death of a Discipline" (reference being to *your* discipline, the discipline of *your* studies), you felt like a like a demented person, wondering about your motives for sticking to your discipline and returning to your alma mater. You have definitely not managed to wean yourself off of your dependency.

But the fact still stands that as students we were all shackled hand and foot. You commenced your studies believing that delight and instruction can go hand in hand: you were put out to pasture under minimal supervision. Just when you were beginning to enjoy yourself, the stranglehold tightened. This pattern repeated itself at every stage. First a perfect balance, *freedom* in *captivity*, then a perversion of both. And when you finally left the university, much reduced in stature, but with a fan of diplomas in your hand, you were yoked together with the rest of this *elite herd* and enlisted in the ranks of the intellectual proletariat. A young Turk I knew saw how things stood with the university. This is what the university has become—he opined—not what it used to be. According to him, an effective form of sabotage of the status quo had to take the guise of self-sabotage. You must pull out at the last moment and unceremoniously refuse your degree with its laughable perquisites. If you are in your right mind, you will refuse the university the satisfaction of having smoothly processed and branded you. You owe this to yourself, because throughout your schooling, in receiving your "priceless" education, you were (unbeknownst to yourself) completing a sophisticated, state-funded course in self-sabotage. Yes, in being beholden to an institution of higher (and highest) learning, you neglected precious *lower learning*. In being encouraged to live exclusively in the world of ideas, you were betraying ideas that entail action. You made a killing doing nothing. Having subjected your ideas (and ideals) to disinterested scholarly inquiry, you denied your ideas (ideals). By being paid to scrutinize your beliefs, you lost the meaning of your beliefs. If this is true, then the ultimate act of defiance against the university will cost you nothing you have not already lost. You will be merely throwing off institutional delusions. Rejecting institutional symbols. Exorcizing institutional evil.

I never followed his advice, and I don't know if he ever did himself. In some respects, I was an exemplar of university education; but in other respects, I was the black sheep of the flock and a long-time dissenter from the university. On the one hand, I have become a prolific writer of academic literature. On the other hand, I am stacking these pages precisely against such literature (and the very notion of "humanistic discipline"!). I am not, of course, disparaging wholesale the work of scholarship, only the complacency of much of the printed knowledge coming out of universities and produced by insecure university employees. This work is all about security. It is only of instrumental use to the individual who produced it. However, regardless of its quality, this literature accumulates in the "knowledge bank" that is the university. You open these scholarly publications— even the very best ones, across the arts and sciences—and you see the glaring instrumentality of the work contained in them. The lazy narrowness of perspective that is truly horrendous, horrendous. The formulaic properties of work that needn't have been formulaic. You get analytical rigor that lacks vigor. You are put to sleep by the paradigm when you could have rallied right on the cutting edge. But, above all, you sense the cutthroat instincts at play. You see scores being settled in footnotes and book reviews. It would be too easy to mistake me for a traitor and malcontent, too easy to accuse me of biting the hand that feeds. Nothing could be further from the truth. The progress of education *really is* hobbled by its own notion of progress. The educational system *is very much* addled by its own notion of system. I have long sensed that the core of the university is rotting away. Where others drool at advances in the Arts and Sciences, I often hold my nose.

Nonetheless, I returned to Poland not long ago fanning myself with my final university diploma. I held in my hand the proof of having sold off the unfettered, autodidactic spirit of true inquiry— that latecomer of a spirit—for a scholar's title. I arrived and, at the first opportunity, worked my way up to the mountains again, wanting to be among them and its people. I stepped into the hillside home of my hosts just as their newborn calf lay dying. The village veterinarian was bedridden and could not examine it. Besides, all the signs read properly were death signs (only backwards could they spell health); an intervention now would be of no use. This ill-timed visit put me in my place. In the solemnity of a late dinner, I was asked for my news and muttered the words "doctor of philosophy." Without looking at the moribund animal, I read the signs backwards and assured them it will get better. The brusque reply I received I can now only paraphrase: "The cow is in a bad way. And the vet is tied up with himself. You might be a doctor, just not the kind we need." To my surprise, these words did not insult me in the least. Thank God for plain speaking! Even among the common folk, the university has lost its good name. Once upon a time, philosophy doctors ranked in usefulness with animal doctors. But now it's a different story.

Fearn Wren

(01.29.08)

To think that you are absent from this book. You, to whom the entire book is addressed, are nowhere to be found in it. Instead, an oblong shadow seen flitting across its pages. I have written to you, written for you—still, I have written you out.

It so happens, my friend, that I am habitually reticent about what I take to be most important. You never hear me mince words about trifles, but do not expect me to tell you what is most important to me. This may sound counterintuitive, but take a good look and you will see that it is exactly true. So I have said nothing, or close to nothing, about you and your work, your work and your art—principles most important to the formation of this book, forming the centre and the circumference by which its other principles are bound like spokes in a wheel. But for you, this book would have spilled into formlessness.

I never intended to get to the crux of the matter, so you cannot accuse me of prevarication. Anything I could say about our extraordinary connection or about your numerous qualities would lack definition and judgment. To say nothing of clairvoyance; I have none in return for my blindness. If an assertion made in delicate matters is not as it should be—dead-on—then it lacks definition and judgment, supplying strife or empty flattery, as the case may be. Even if the relationship between you and this book was a lucid one—I am speaking here of the book's relation to you as well as your relations with the book—I would be at a loss for words to delineate it. As it is, I have only an impression of how things stand between you. As things stand, this work has not even fully come to terms with itself *as a book*, much less a book written to you. On the one hand, it is motivated by your unsigned permission to exist; your silence shepherds it into being. On the other hand, it knows itself to be breaking the rules; this unruliness makes it what it is.

Sooner or later, however, the work must come around to the

book. I know how to be patient and how to wait. I began cultivating patience in thinking out of consideration not for myself and the *success* of my thinking, but for what I think about and pursue in my thought. Over the years, I might have turned this patient thinking into a solitary game—one which I usually play to the end, and frequently win, and whose rules I occasionally rewrite, though not before I had played against the rules, broken them many times over (when they no longer seemed fair or right or whatever), and de facto replaced them with their violations. But for all my patient thinking, I find myself at the absolute weakest point in life. The weakest and, at the same time, highest point. It is as though in waiting I have been giving in to the way things are (to the way I wished they weren't), without confronting or transforming them. Except that all I do is confront and transform them in my mind, all I think about is confronting and transforming, taking them head-on . . .

By writing to you from within my demoralized state—just when it is at its most pronounced and compromising—I seem to be working towards a solution. If I tell myself I am working towards a solution, I must really be working towards one. Haven't I channeled all my thoughts into finding it? Well then I must already be thinking of it. The relation of the book's parts to the book as a whole is such that each part both clarifies and obscures the whole, just as the whole both clarifies and obscures each part. All is animated through shifting patterns of light and shadow. The solution of this work, taking us beyond this work, lies beyond its clarities and obscurities. For an instant (easy to miss) everything will be dissolved, voided: what needs to be remembered will be remembered and what forgotten, forgotten; the guilt, the doubt, the confusion will be put to rest; the torment will be over. Then everything will begin all over again.

But for the time being, I have an address, I know the door; I knock on this door when no-one is in, and someone is known to open them after I've left. If my writing is anything in real-life terms, it is this blessed spate of missed encounters. Were we to ever meet in person, this book would quantify the silences between us. That in itself could be another book (another impossible conversation). For my part, I would have exhausted myself with this work and would have little else to say about my ties to it. I might be wearing light summer clothes that day, but they would signify mourning— because, of course, I would have by then buried this book (which I should not hesitate to call *our book*). This work would have taken everything out of me; I would be finished, you see, eking out a post-humous existence.

It might be sunny that day, I might have plenty of *joie de vivre*. Wearing the same light clothes (signifying the opposite of mourn-ing), I might walk to our meeting place hoping it to be a place free of literature and cinema. Literature and cinema too quickly go to one's head. Don't you find that within minutes of absorbing their atmosphere—and especially their *joint* atmosphere—there is noth-ing outside of literature and cinema anymore; that every comment and observation must be filtered through either cinema or literature, or preferably both, to count at all? They are no less forms of flight from ourselves and our realities for being extensions of ourselves and our unrealities—I hasten to add, of our most cherished unrealities. Perhaps I exaggerate slightly, but that is only to highlight the *per-nicious social effects* of cinema and literature . . . So I would much rather meet you in a place in which nature dictates conversation. For instance trees. Trees have the power to turn a banal conversation into a one-of-a-kind kind of conversation. Trees, the qualities and mean-ing of trees. The august simplicity and quiet grandeur of some trees.

Alternatively (there are obviously infinite alternatives): shadows and their variations. The eerie cast of tree shadows at certain angles and elevations.

There are so many things I could ask you and tell you about trees and shadows. Even if we were sitting amid tall buildings at noon, we would still be *in nature, in shadow*. Then and there, with this idle chat, the living memory of our fellowship and solitude would be erased. We might still be able to read about them in this book, but our memory would appear washed out in the face of this newly resplendent reality. So why would we go back, reopen the book, hold it up to reality? You might say: you had my fellowship, it was real, only I could not tell you about it. I hoped so, I might reply, this was the kind of solitude I wanted to give you. But such hindsight, such afterwords, would have no bearing on the present: on my sense of solitary fellowship (or the intensity of this sense), on my passion for writing and my obsession with it (or the intensity of this passion-cum-obsession). For all my pensive forays into a hypothetical future—who can resist them when on one's last legs?—I am still up to my neck in everything; I might be thinking ahead and thinking beyond this quagmire of a book, but meanwhile I am still wading through it.

When all is said and done, this work may only be redeemed as a runaway homage to you. This may again sound counterintuitive, since I seem to be writing of nothing but myself; but take another look and you will realize I have written of everything but myself—that, as a matter of fact, I have distilled myself without scruple into a sort of spirit hovering above these pages. I have often said (or implied) that this is a passionate and fugitive work. But it was Hoffer who said: "The passionate pursuer has all the earmarks of a fugitive." So this is a work about escape and pursuit. It might require detours through checkered pasts and specious reasoning, but pursuit is paramount among them, and escape is the closest thing to its *raison d'être*. Similarly, it may be carried out through a web of events, encounters, and ideas centered on my person, but escape, for which pursuit is the best rationale, is nonetheless paramount among them. Everything addressed in this book is methodically plotted along this double vector of escape and pursuit, of refuge and passion. It is between you and me, this work, and about neither.

Fearn Wren

(03.12.08)

Some say solitude is like death. And, then and there, they take to demonstrating their skill in living. It does not even occur to them, the fools, that they are busy at such demonstrating three hundred and sixty five days of the year. They get one day in a leap year for living, one *leap of life*, and the rest of the time they are demonstrating, merely pretending to live and making a royal mess of it, pretending instead of living it. But they have the nerve to say that *my* solitude is deathly, that it reeks of interment, that it is all just memories and books—memories with which I have shrouded myself and books with which I have immured myself—and that the tales I spin, *my* tales, are "just tales from a crypt."

Someone dies and we say: a life has been *extinguished*. Not all of us use that very word, but most think of life as a flame snuffed out by death. To witness someone dying is as though to witness a fire being put out. There is energy—the heat of the body, the glow of the face, radiant smiles and gleaming eyes—and suddenly all is cold and dark. "Life is a pure flame, and we live by an invisible Sun within us" (Browne). We die when our "inner light" goes out like a furnace flame (without even having seen in). We cease to be and leave others in the dark about ourselves. We leave them in the dark and in the cold, until they learn to get on without us. Sometimes we wonder if an outside force is not perhaps seeking to extinguish us, then wash away all trace of us. It may be that we are burning up from the inside and the flames need putting out.

There is no-one alive who can tell me about the child in that photograph: who it was or, rather, whose it was. It is not that I obsess over it. The infant is no different from all the other infants entrusted to their graves in all the world's villages, in the penumbra of all the world's cities. The soil is turned over them and they just about vanish. Nary a trace of them. Just images of an inchoate someone, haunting the parent or parents with its prodigious potential. Only the parents',

only the mother's, trauma: the infant like an acute trauma, like a
wound through the womb. Hysterical memories. But with the dirt
of life turned over them, they vanish. The parent of a recently dead
child is cut off from poetry. She or he might wish, might reach for
poetry, but is cut off from it. (Is a child in the ground really a cherub
in heaven?)

All infants make but *one blot*, you realize as you weave through
the cemetery. Adults are inscribed with biographies, but infants did
not live long enough to have biographies. (Both, however, are blot-
ted out by history, you note as you linger in the military section
of the cemetery, then in the children's section.) Unlike the epitaphs
and portraits of adults, the sparse inscriptions on the gravestones of
infants give you nothing to go on, leave nothing to the imagination,
raise no questions. Each infant grave is a yawning abyss; you are
reminded by it of the absence of memory, the tenuousness of meaning. Whenever I pass over these graves or stop to stare into them,
I am nagged by such thoughts. There is no individual here, only a
lump of flesh inside a hole (back inside a hole). My imagination is
stretched just by imagining a bereaved family, a family crying over
this piece of flesh. If I never visit my little half-sister's grave it is to
keep myself from thinking of her as a little flesh in the ground. I keep
reminding myself of her little soul and her share of physical suffering.
It is essential that I keep thinking of both her soul and physical suffering together. If I thought just of the suffering, I would stumble,
mentally stumble, over the *physical* part. The disgrace of the physical. When I think of the souls of dead children, especially of dead
infants, rarely do I think of heaven and salvation. Usually, I think of
limbo and perdition. I remember the *no bitterness on earth hence no
sweetness in heaven* line from Mickiewicz's *Forefathers*. I tell myself:
do what pagan Slavs did, give them some mustard seed to get them
into heaven. Then I think: what nonsense!

My lifelong obsession with death (also my strongest "philosophical" obsession) has to do with the fact that when I celebrate my

birthday everyone heads for the cemetery. On every one of my birthdays I was diverted from a commemoration of my own birth to a commemoration of the death of others. My parents never failed to wrap up the birthday festivities to get on with the deathday festivities. Alright, they would say, you had your party, let's all now go to the cemetery. Just when my life was on the agenda, I was led to a place where lives lived dwindled to piles of stones and memories. One went there to think of those lives but left with a headful of death. And I—I began that day with my mind on the *terminus a quo*, but always ended it on the *terminus ad quem*.

As most of the family had been buried outside the capital, and trips outside the capital were a rare affair, my parents and I would end up strolling through the city's historic cemetery with no-one to visit. It was never more than a symbolic observance. Cemeteries were the place to be, so they elected the most impressive cemetery. The main avenue, side alleys, and manicured crossings between them, the swell of tinted candlelight lifting the darkness, the scent of fresh chrysanthemums, the visitors kneeling in prayer or tidying up the graves—the cemetery grounds on All Souls' Day evoked an outdoor cathedral. On All Souls' Day, it lived up to its saccharine name *garden of remembrance*; wilted on an average day, its memories reblossomed. One could roam through this cathedral-garden and forget about one's existence. So naturally I grew to like those *cemetery birthday outings*. Through the coupling of occasions, I began to identify with the cemetery—first with this festive cemetery, then with any old cemetery. More and more, I associated those grave walks with myself; if initially they had nothing to do with me, they gradually came to have everything to do with me.

Grappling with thoughts of death has been my great preoccupation for some time now. I have never been able to settle on a stance towards death—mine or anybody else's. A large share of my mental life consists in this *seesawing* between different mindsets towards death. I used to imagine, for instance, that if I only thought of myself as *an animal*, the thought of death would become bearable to me; I would still be saddled with death, but not ridden by it. Just as if I thought of myself as *an individual*, my solitude would (and did) become livable, instead of always threatening to become unlivable. But until now I have not managed to think of myself as an animal. It is not because of any existential or spiritual conflicts. After all, one could resign from humanity and still follow humanity. One could create the "new animal" in place of the "new man." And one would still have the *anima* in *animal*. But, given the prevailing connotations of animality, it is really a most difficult thing for a human being to take themselves for an *animal being*. One can be an animal and never once feel an animal. One can feel inhuman, or be dehumanized, and not feel animalized. One can live like an animal (a so-called savage existence) and feel fully human. One can act a savage and think oneself super-human. No state seems conducive to thinking of oneself as an animal so as to face death and demystify it. No other state than a sick one—a *zoanthropic* state, a human sickness called animal—to cheat death from behind or from below. In illness only do we feel more animal than man, but the animal in us is *mal*; it is not a creature open to being, free from death, but one sick with premonition of non-being. At best, one imagines death as shedding one's animal skin while cleaving to one's human soul (which only mystifies it further). Or one thinks of death as a lot shared with animals, as leveling one to an animal (which makes it degrading). For such an *animal death* to become bearable, one must have led an animal life, thought oneself an animal, been reclaimed by nature, and so on.

A recent news brief on so-called pauper burials made me think of the bodies that go unclaimed in our province. But the number of such bodies (in Quebec running annually into the hundreds) is high enough for their burial to have become a problem. Although the province inherits all unclaimed estates, the few funeral homes that do bury paupers get but a pittance for their service. Government funding pays for a simple casket, a group grave, and a ground marker with a number on it. Cremation, or even the humblest of obsequies, are too costly. "For the amount of money they give," complained the head of Quebec funeral direc-tors, "there's nothing, let's say sweet, that is done, or can be done."

I once believed the worst death to be death by water, the most abject funeral, a watery one. If immolation was for the spiritually strong, drowning was for the spiritually weak. Not even Jules Verne's depiction of a funeral at the bottom of the sea—which remained with me because of its *eerie humanism*— made desirable a "moist relentment." To have for a grave a sodden hole beneath the waves seemed to me utterly forlorn. But "Captain Nobody" sought out such forlornness. One needed time to appreci-ate his philosophy. "'Yes, forgotten by all else, but not by us,'" he said of a man just buried. Was there ever a more otherworldly sepulture? Some hundred feet below the surface, by the submerged light of elec-tric lanterns, a group of early aquanauts inter the body of a dead companion, marking the site with a cross of red coral like "petri-fied blood." "'We dug the grave,'" said the Captain, "'and the polypi undertake to seal our dead for eternity.'" But the coral (the animal called coral) undertakes no such thing. Its tentacles remove the death shroud, its mouths remove the flesh. The bones become the skeleton of the reef. Meanwhile, the coral cross loses its cruciform shape. Soon no trace of the grave remains. Small fish feed on the coral, sharks feed on the fish, men of course prey on the sharks, and so the dead were not out of the reach of "sharks and *men*" after all. Everything always ends in some dissolution. Even the universe—an idea floated by Blanqui, who saw in the Sun a star in decline. "A day will come [for] the end of the reign of flames and the beginning of that of the aqueous vapors, where the sea will have the last word." And it will douse the world, put out its living daylights.

The other day, I found myself on a bus eavesdropping on two men. Gauging from their gestures and where they later got off, they must have been patients of the municipal mental health system. It was a very cogent exchange, albeit mostly in monologue, with one man doing the talking, the other the listening. The speaker held forth on the "quality of life" in medieval Europe—specifically, on disparities in the quality of life between medieval cities and villages and on how the Black Death "obliterated" those disparities. The listener kept nodding away, mum save for a sporadic "yeah" of encouragement, but who could tell whether he cared much for this topic or merely enjoyed his own silence. I, meanwhile, became engrossed in the man's discourse, for one because of its obscurity and passion, which carried over into his discussion of modern life. In the last snippet I am able to recall of it, he spoke of electricity as the root of all evil and essentially *against nature*. On this point he reached a frenetic eloquence, employing words like "scourge" and "grave" and "catastrophic." I cannot remember his exact turns of phrase, because by that time I had already lost interest—he suddenly appeared to me to be completely out of his mind, and, besides, not all inflated rhetoric works its magic upon me. I do, however, recall some of my own thoughts, which took off from his in a wholly unusual direction.

First off, it occurred to me that death is more dramatic by fire light. That, in the uneven conditions afforded by torches and bonfires, with a darkness pierced only by flames, death is reasoned away as divine justice or natural law. That it (death) could not survive as a *ritual* by the artifice of electric light. Lenin predicted electricity would replace divinity and it did. Then again, as a *routine* death reaps in the broadest daylight. In fire light, I began again, murder becomes *much more conceivable*. In low lighting, one is drawn to murderousness and thievery as a way of life. In a world lit only by natural light, murder becomes a rite of passage from a law-governed diurnal existence to a lawless nocturnal existence. One could cite city-wide blackouts as evidence of the contrary: that overriding darkness inspires not enmity and looting, but camaraderie and sharing. But this is only, one could parry, because of a *collective expectation of light*. The system never stops running, supported in the interim by a slew of emergency generators. The expectation of light is an expectation of punishment.

In a dire situation (say, a wide-ranging natural disaster, a doomsday situation) where no-one expects the power to come on, murder, rape, and looting become not only collectively thinkable, but contagious. People rapidly become aware of the primal appetites stirring within them. The unreconciled, the insulted, the mentally unstable, the vagrant, and the penurious, who have nothing to gain from light, are the first to take advantage of darkness. And who can blame them? Even paragons of virtue, whose business does not require the cover of night, who want for nothing and who at the moment bear no grudge against reality, would with time, watching their neighbors devolve into bandits, seeing that need is not just the mother of ingenuity, or feeling their own needs getting out of hand, be swept away by the general atavism. Even such virtuous men and women, I am willing to wager, would lapse into vice and revert to the law of the jungle and hunger for one another. It is only societies *emerging* from darkness, societies which do not take light (the law of light) for granted, that could keep themselves afloat during an extended outage. Whereas a modern society, a society accustomed to the continuous flow of power, would be plunged into chaos.

The death of society is worse than the death of an individual. The death of society carries with it the death of the individual. In society (in the principle of society) the individual finds their salvation, he/she is not lost, and certainly not dead or given up for dead. To accuse solitary individuals of shunning society, or to say "I am shunning society as a solitary individual," is absurd. It is not against nature to shun society; quite the opposite. To shun society is to give oneself up to nature without a fight. But to be received by nature with our dignity unscathed, we must always put up a fight. Because nature is indifferent to us and, if we surrender, it will be oblivious to our suffering and sacrifice. Nature must fill us with horror, even as we tend towards it. It is natural that it should fill us with horror; its voraciousness is beyond all imagination and it shows but few signs of partiality to us. So we must not let ourselves simply be swallowed up by nature. Because when we are swallowed up by it—figuratively swallowed up by it—we are as good as dead. We renounce ourselves, and by renouncing ourselves we are killing ourselves. We claim to have no attachments to society, nothing to let go of, nothing to take our leave of. I will not believe any individual has truly shunned society, truly renounced themselves, permanently and unequivocally. This is a myth, I think. We are a part of nature, we succumb to nature, but in our humanity are always against nature. By putting up a fight against nature, I do not mean violence; I mean disobedience. Violence directed at nature is violence upon our own nature. I do believe we can have humankind without violence. Once we take humanity into our own hands we will *engineer* violence out of it. We will have a docile humanity, a toothless humanity if you will, but we shall have civilization. Throughout all these barbaric millennia we were dreaming of civilization, and finally we shall have it. From our new vantage point, we shall look back upon all our so-called ancient and modern civilizations as we do upon the progress of troglodytes.

Fearn Wren

(04.04.08)

When thinking of inspiration, we often think along and past it: of expiration. Through inspiration to expiration, I always used to say, though stopped saying because it sounded dour. The meanings of *spirit*, breath, the vital nature of this breath, *spiritus*, air, the idea of expiring, of giving up the spirit, all suggest that life itself is one continual inspiration. Yet the ups and downs of mental life, the hilly nature of thinking, have us calling *inspiration* only the peaks in this terrain, turning the valleys into lulls through which one drifts dispiritedly, as though asleep. As soon as the spirit reaches its immaterial maximum, one begins dying. Your lifespan depends, so to speak, on your existential lungs; how long before they are fully expanded and exhaustion sets in by degrees? As Novalis says somewhere, absolute equality is the highest work of art, but it is unnatural. Some are born with a set of gills, whereby they extract air from the most inhospitable environment; others have seemingly unlimited pulmonary capacity to survive until some puncture brings an end to them; others again can hold their breath with the endurance of a free diver. Their respective works reflect nature's inequality. When I think of inspiration in this way—it would seem in the most fatalistic, self-defeating way—I also think of the lifespan of ideas. I am reminded of the terrible days when the birth of an idea implies the death of that idea. When inspiration appears rather as expiration. Every year, even every month, I hit such a bad patch in my thinking, where all my thoughts leading up to it are overturned. I have not yet learned to harness inspiration, so every such instance is something of a little death to me. Everything about me sinks to a dangerously low level. It has always been on again, off again between me and inspiration. Typical of a manic-depressive personality, one might add. The manic phase often (though not often enough) feels like inspiration, while the depressive phase often (*all too* often) feels like expiration, lending itself easily to analogies with death.

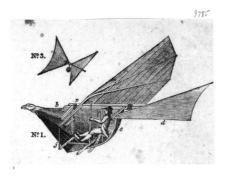

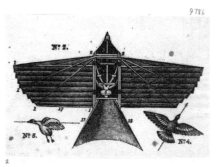

In my childhood, I was completely obsessed with flight (I am, by the way, no longer obsessed with it). And it is flying that I, like most people, think of when I *imagine* and indeed experience inspiration. I was never interested in airplanes, ballooning, parachuting, or even hang gliding, but in bird flight, and by extension in the migration of birds and in the bird's perspective. I drew flying suits that mimicked nature, disguising the flier as a gigantic bird. Only recently I was reminded of those meticulous sketches (now long lost) by a design of sounder engineering in Leonardo's *Codex* and the lesser Alexander Anderson's scrapbook, or, again, on a plate from Goya's *Disparates*. In my literal and lively pursuit of flight I was inspired by a leaden (!) statuette of Icarus; it was all the proof I needed that a pair of wings is outfit enough to be airborne. I jumped off of many a roof in attempts to defy gravity; I stood flapping my arms sometimes for hours over a map spread out on the floor; I dreamt of flying over my entire district like an aerial land surveyor. I only mention these infantile foibles—for that is what they were—to show that I imagined and felt what inspiration can be like long before experiencing it directly. Or perhaps I experienced it in an adumbrated sense. I would not know true inspiration for many years thence, but this childhood obsession must have been some presentiment of it.

Now, when one speaks of being inspired, it is most often with a mind to execute something. (To say *I am inspired* to no end is like saying *I am alive*, though most people think of life as a spiritual burden instead of a spiritual gift.) The object and particulars of the execution may still be vague—one feature of inspiration I have observed in myself is the initial lack of focus on the logistics of execution—but one already has either a salient detail or an overall idea of what is to be done. The elation one feels seems to be contingent on the openness of possibilities. Even as one is motivated by their execution, certain of the execution, has absolute trust in oneself as the executor, and absolute trust that what is to be executed is worthy of being so. But to return to flight—the dream of flight, the *will to flight*—one is inspired (in one's inspiration) by the flight itself and by what one sees during the flight, by the bird's-eye view of things. It is therefore disheartening when a flight—by which I mean a *flight of fancy*—comes to an abrupt end, as it almost always does in my case: *abruptly*. If you can believe it, in the past months I have just as often written myself out of depression (and into mania) as I have written myself into depression (and out of mania). That moment in which one's writing takes a turn for the worse is virtually imperceptible and, for this reason alone, cannot be forestalled; very possibly I am among the few who do not perceive the switch before it is too late. I have come to call this ineluctable turn my *augenblick*. This German word has always appealed to me; even before I made it mine, made it *my augenblick*, I would refer to abrupt changes of any kind as augenblicks, if not in conversation, then in my own mind. Then I began applying the word to the flame-like leaps of the spirit from one extreme to the other. In fact, when I began to write this note to you, I thought I had just experienced one of these split-second reversals. In the case of mania and depression one is justified in using the word *reversal*; periods in which neither mania nor depression dominate become irrelevant, playing no part in the creative process—they are periods of mental stagnation as far as I am concerned (at least in the case of my current work), periods characterized neither by inspiration nor expiration but plain old respiration, by doing only to undo, by not being able to strike a spark from one's surroundings with one's brain—they are indeed periods of zero-sum economy, when the mind simply seizes up under the pressure of intellection. One quickly uses up one's reserves of mental energy in oscillating between manic and depressive writing, and in between them (if one is granted an in-between) one is mentally and emotionally comatose. It is a time not just of ennui (or something close to ennui) and listlessness, but of subtly mounting worry; as the lack of productivity becomes more and more worrisome, even the hair on your head is worried by your restless fingers, you break out in a cold sweat in anticipation of complete mental paralysis. And before you know it, you have slipped into despondent ruminations about the future of your guiding idea, the execution of your plan. Pretty soon you have thought yourself into a depressive state, which feels like no other depression before it; it is simply the deepest and lowest state you've plummeted to, the lowest and perhaps the longest—a terminal state. Writing is still possible, but it is nothing like what most people think writing to be; it is like gasping for air. You vent your anguish in bursts of words. Were it not for this shortness of breath, you would howl; but howling does not become a writer, one does not become a writer by howling.

Then writing starts to flow again out of panic: a panic-stricken writing. One pulls out the map—the map of the area one had been moving through—to find one's place on this map. Then throws a quick glance at the schedule (adding to the panic), to consult the schedule on one's timing—perhaps one was mistaken in the calculations, perhaps one can still get to where one was going on time, if not ahead of time. A rising sense of doom inspires you to rush headlong without thinking, and in an augenblick you are moved to make up for lost time, to exert yourself to the utmost to overcome the distance still separating you from your destination, and this breathless confidence in your abilities produces another type of writing—the manic type—altogether different in character, with a lot going for it, notably happiness. But let not *that* be your be-all-and-end-all. Inflammation of the mind, even drawing on inspiration, quickly burns itself out. Dissipation of the mind is sure to follow, etcetera. When writing becomes an onrush of words, when it becomes automatic (and you cease to feel a connection with it), you know it is high time to desist. I am interested in these emotional swings only when I have hit the middle register in exasperation. Not because I need to dissect the mechanism behind them, not because I want to control them, but because a mind so preoccupied with itself cannot fail to inquire into its own modi operandi.

Composing a work boils down to creating favorable and even extreme conditions for the emergence of an idea and the precipitation of that idea. Real physical and physiological conditions for tapping into one's inspiration or, indeed, the lack thereof. All day yesterday I carried in my head the intention to write, but could not find the right conditions for it. I could not even tell if I was under the influence of inspiration. Fed up, around four o'clock, I made my way to the Centre for the History of the Book, where for the next few hours I waited and then listened to a public talk by a world-famous scholar professing to break the pattern of *euphoria* and *depression* about the future of the book. He promised to make a "sober," "philosophical" intervention into this "bipolar prophesying" prevalent in academic circles, but achieved little more than an inventory of existing ideas—without pushing the question of the future of the book far enough to really "make a difference." In his closing statement, he paraphrased Wilhelm von Humboldt—the university is the only institutional place where the different tonalities of the different enthusiasms of different generations can inspire each other—which later sent me in search of Humboldt's memorandum of 1810. The lecture ended, a poor man's reception commenced in a darkling room, whose only appointment, besides a table and rows of empty shelving, was a maquette of the building we stood in (appendaged to the main library), and within a quarter of an hour the last of the lecture's attendees had dispersed. I, too, promptly left the place, which with each passing minute became physically more oppressive, as I imagined the scale model containing this same room with another miniature of itself, and so on into infinity. I headed over to the book stacks to escape this boxed-in feeling, which bodes poorly for inspiration, to browse through some of the titles mentioned during the lecture. Strange, I reflected on the tram ride back, how much I worked to get inside the university, putatively erected in the Romantic vein—upon freedom and isolation—and where the entire world unrolled itself like a map, as it must to birds in flight. Now— after years of opening doors and closing them quietly behind me—I am left with the abstract sensation of standing inside one of those Chinese boxes, which as you know contain only smaller and smaller versions of themselves. On getting home, I dipped into Humboldt's writings and found it inspiring fare.

There is a fuller and more immediate effectiveness of a great spirit than that possible through his works. These show only a part of his being. The entirety flows pure and wholly through his living personal self . . . Written works—literatures—then take it mummified, as it were, over those gaps which the living effectiveness can no longer leap . . . However great certain thoughts and works might be, it is hard to bear when the human being seems to disappear in them, when the truth of feeling is sacrificed to the artistic product, when the person yields himself completely to his work with an egotism that can't be gainsaid.

I woke up the next morning just as the Good Friday pageant began drawing small knots of people outside my house. Year in year out, I have been the involuntary spectator of this fervent re-enactment of the passion, crucifixion and entombment of Christ, which glides just past my window and is entirely framed by it like a moving picture. I always soak up the drama in spite myself and, exactly like last year, stood inside looking out and hearing the frills of fanfare, the plaintive song of old women clad in raven-black, the intermittent barking of Roman soldiers as they flogged the Son of God down this narrow street. As the parade wound its way around the bend, I caught the last glimpse of a life-size effigy of the Messiah lying in state on a catafalque, which inexplicably was my cue to resume this note.

I have kept up this work despite many difficulties, and it is not my only work (one has many irons in the fire). But neither is it of a piece with the others. When I feel the urge to write it, I follow through with the urge. Even though I type my way across white pages using my hands, my advance resembles tramping through new snow like a pioneer. There is normally no time for backtracking or idleness in this legwork, and my only stops are rest-stops, when I look back on that stretch of work with gratification. Whenever I think of footsteps and footprints in relation to writing, I am spirited away to the blank landscape described with a few deft strokes of the pen at the start of *Kolyma Tales*. A handful of prisoners tread shoulder-to-shoulder through deep snow in the wake of the "narrow, wavering track of the first man." To rest, he lies down on the snow and lights a hand-rolled cigarette. "[T]he tobacco smoke hangs suspended above the white, gleaming snow like a blue cloud. The man moves on, but the cloud remains hovering above the spot where he rested," like a thought or afterthought—"for the air is motionless" on days chosen for beating down roads, where "tractors and horses driven by readers, instead of authors and poets," will soon be passing. Shalamov's opening parable does not elicit pity for those who perished in the enormous penal colony of Kolyma. One feels this is not its intention. Instead, the story touches the quiddity of writing, which its author, a gulag survivor, chose to allegorize with rare circumspection as the prisoners' routine toil.

If one has leisure to write, one may be tempted to defer the pleasure of setting to work, or one may actually set to work without delay. Anyone who has tried it knows that the first is perilous for serious undertakings. Not to be confused with procrastination, it means accomplishing those mundane tasks that have already been delayed before and are less urgent. Small pleasures can now be had from them—they give a foretaste of the greater pleasure just set aside. In reality, one buries the opportunity to make the most of one's inspiration by following a mere distraction, which is always part of a *diversionary chain*: one diversion leading to the next. (Eventually one's pace slackens, inspiration goes out the window, and nothing remarkable gets done.) But the second scenario—rolling up one's sleeves and staring forthwith—is also not without its perils, and can, in certain persons, invite unmerited pretension. One shuts oneself off from external influences that (again, in certain persons) help offset the almost monomaniacal tendency to pursue one's work at the expense of everything else. There is, I nearly forgot, a third way, the most suicidal. It is the urge to close in on one's inspiration, to get to the meat of one's inspiration in an unnatural way, through a mental shortcut rather than through the process of writing as such. Instead of letting the inspiration carry you on its wings, you stick a pin through it as though it were dead.

When one is inspired and working away, one hardly ever stops. I work best under conditions of moderate freedom and isolation. Nighttime lucubrations, which keep one indoors and sever them from the rest of humanity, are not for me. When all is quiet and dark, I stare at a wall because of its brightness, because with my eyes on this wall my head can clear, if only for a moment. But before it has a chance to clear, an ant appears on the wall. A black carpenter ant, you notice, is making its way up the wall. You remember that everything beneath your feet is rotting, possibly the entire structure of this house is haven to an orgy of ants, excavating their galleries below the threshold of audibility. They have been here before you arrived on the scene, and have begun emerging out of the woodwork just to show you they are the primary tenants. Or I play a piece of music, because the relative silence opens up the channels for the omnipresent buzz of electricity, raising more mental confusion than the whir of an engine, and I place my hopes in this piece of music to pick up or prolong my inspiration—but the music only proves an interference, yet another, often a major one, and one knows better not to play anything. Anything but. Better deaf for the work's sake than in thrall to "inspirational" music like sonata no. 32 op. 111. The only exception to this rule, the only piece that neither interferes nor is interfered with but complements contrapuntally my thinking and my writing, must be "Sleep Walk." If the phonographic needle followed the grooves of my brain, my skull would resonate with the slides and swells of this melody. I have played "Sleep Walk" with undue frequency, played it like no other melody, and still have not overplayed it. The purity of the steel guitar has been lost through magnetic deterioration, but something else has been gained in the process: a fundamental attunement between this musical composition and my thoughts, which ensures that I'll never outgrow it. I play "Sleep Walk"—by far the best tune on the 1959 American charts and one of the most unwhistleable tunes of all time—until I can no longer listen to anything; but when I feel ready for music again, when I find myself craving music, it is "Sleep Walk" that I crave; "The Red Pony" also comes to mind, but I don't put it on. It won't do without tuning, and even then it goes only tolerably well. You might judge based on this that I am musically impoverished. It would be truer to say that I am a musical abstinent—and have become one on account of my work.

The idea of writing to you was conceived shortly after my encounter with you and your work. Having seen your work and heard your thoughts about it, having seen you bring into correspondence the obscurity of language and the clarity of things, I felt a surge of inspiration. On the one hand, to rethink the work I do, to turn my work outwards, to radically alter the quite predictable fate of my work, and, on the other, to forge a "direct connection" with you through my work, through the habitude of work. While you sat conversing with the person closest to me, my closest friend for a long time,

I stood aside to lay down the cornerstone for this book; without actually thinking of writing a book, I stood by conceiving of both the connection and the work that would become this book. I did not join the two of you because I subconsciously understood the necessity of keeping my distance from you, of relinquishing contact with you in that fortuitous and ordinary way to have reason to move towards you in this radical and extraordinary way. Without any connection to you to speak of—only a barely established connection to your work—I was already distancing myself from you in preparation for approaching you. I held myself back from speaking an unpremeditated word to you as a pretext for writing a whole host of well-thought-out words later on. I say "I held myself back" because a part of me did not seek distance and was drawn to the certain ordinary proximity with you; but my other, stronger part would be satisfied only with uncertain, extra-ordinary proximity. I write "I" in reference to "myself" back then, but the person I was then is now a stranger to me. I cannot speak for that person who took steps away from you, despite being heir to their legacy of distance. Were I faced with you now, looking into me as you did then (which gives me the sneaking suspicion that you must have known what I would do before I myself knew it), I would not pass up another opportunity for ordinary proximity to you because of the extra-ordinary distance that has been developing between us ever since the start of our written connection.

The following month I went on a driving tour of New England with my father and half-brother. My seventy-two-year-old father and my half-brother, recently come of age, had together flown over from Poland to America especially to make the trip. I decided to go with them, which is to say, to be driven around by them in that exquisite part of America—and, at the same time, to withdraw from them and from my own reality to focus, as much as possible (as much as the scenery allowed me to), on thoughts of my encounter with your work and the creative possibilities stemming from that encounter. In other words, I turned a unique occasion to get to know this father and brother, a new reality of being at close quarters with them both, into an occasion for exploring my imagination, whose sole outlet now became this book.

I made a rather surly travel companion. The truth was that after putting myself in this family situation I was desperate to escape it, and since I could not physically escape it, I escaped it mentally. The way into this book was therefore my way out, my ingress into an egress. The book certainly had the power to take my mind off of things. The motivation of those first precipitate steps inside the book had, in my view, riddled the design of the book, turning it into a maze for losing oneself in. My bred-in-the-bone egotism and the anti-familial sentiments I nurture, which incidentally run in the family but are heightened in me by my physical distance from my family, always conquer my rectitude. I can go back as far as memory allows and always see myself treating the family as an abominable imposture, against which those whose nature is opposed to it are ultimately defenseless. I associate family relations (sad to say) with monetary benefits, which I almost see as (never quite adequate) compensation for remaining in touch with the family. Any other benefits seem to me to be accidental or offered so grudgingly that their personal value depreciates to zero. Day-to-day family life has for me consisted of more or less mechanical and disingenuous interactions, and the families I had a chance to study only reinforced my perceptions. (I have yet to meet a family that does not conceal its emotional brutality. As a rule, the most toxic families put up the best appearance for the outsider, whom they have invited in—but there comes a point sure as daylight when they brand the outsider [now an insider] an intruder. Such families hold together remarkably well because of their internal and external bad blood.) My perceptions of my actual family members are either one-dimensional and negative or tinged with apathy (my chain-smoking alcoholic grandmother, my cantankerous grandmother, my curmudgeonly grandfather, my alcoholic aunt, my splenetic half-sister. . .you get the point). Of all my family members, I have been the most consistently successful at defending myself against family and the principle of the family. As far as I am concerned, I do not take after *those people*. I have what one might call a great familial need, but it is misdirected—that is, directed away from my actual family to family-surrogates—which somehow negates it. I will always be a migratory bird, and every year or so I will fly back to my family for a period, despite becoming increasingly estranged from it, and then return to a reality in which family relations figure as minimal dialogues relayed by telephone. But here we were, the three of us, breaking of our habitual patterns of interaction, which obviously discombobulated us. Our discomfort made the whole escapade precarious and potentially volatile. We remained assiduously reserved, our exchanges limited to directions and arguments about where we were going.

All this, of course, weighed heavily on my mind and naturally took my mind off the book. The more I insisted on thinking of the book, weighing the possibility and impossibility of it, the more improbable it appeared, which only fanned my interest in the idea, until again it began to smolder. I kept up this toing and froing throughout Vermont, New Hampshire, Maine, Massachusetts, and Connecticut. Most of all, I thought of it in Atlantic City, trapped between day and night in that terminal gamblers' town. The bleached promenade and sterile beaches, the white surf, have long ceased to compete with the casinos. So bare was this strip, so treeless, that inadvertently one took cover in the *Taj Mahal* or *Caesars*, where colors regained their saturation. The contrast favored the older of these haunts, which, as the eyes adjusted to their gilded splendor and opulent kitsch, revealed their decline. One imagined their maintenance has long been limited to vacuuming and air-freshening. I also noticed with sadness that what once symbolized the visceral thrill of winning—the shower of coins into their metal trays—was not to be heard; instead, synthetic sounds, issuing from a hundred machines, multiplied by a scheme of mirrors, brought on the image of some millennial exhibition hall full of robots obnoxiously vying for human attention. My mind, otherwise unoccupied with the here and now, roamed free for a good three hours—the length of our dour stroll—and I registered only the names of certain eateries—*Gold Tooth Gertie's, Fortunes, Gatsby's, Poker Snack Bar*—and such things as seemed ironic or out of place, like a storefront psychic or the fact that the rickshaw drivers were, almost to a man, young Poles. After leaving Atlantic City that same evening, we headed for New York and the most productive period of my contemplation of the work to come.

Permission

The moment I set foot in midtown Manhattan, I resolved to take it in with the wonderment of a child. I understood that with this city there were no half measures. I struck out early every morning, covering mile after mile with the meticulousness of a land surveyor and devotion of a religious zealot. I finally understood the notion of *arteries* when applied to a city's infrastructure: the steady flow of its lifeblood, the circulation of denizens and tourists. Each district had its own distinct blood pressure and pulse. For the short while I was in New York, I was awestruck. Everything projected and poured itself into my eye sockets. From the bowels of the subway system, through the patched-up pavements, to the tips that nothing touches, save birds perhaps—and I, walking and minding only these heights, had stepped on a lifeless sparrow that had also not minded its sights—all was accident upon accident in this city where apparent chaos resolved itself into perfect order, a city I have long dreamt of seeing again.

If I like a place and want to return there, I visit its public library. Where other tourists toss coins into fountains, I apply for a member's card. The membership soon expires, but this personal memento is a reminder of my affection for a city, and the eventual renewal of membership signifies the continuity of that affection. My visit to the New York Public Library was for this very purpose. Prior to registration, I usually familiarized myself with a library's holdings, the conditions of its reading room, and the rights granted to its members. This time around, such thorough inspection was the furthest thing from my mind, most of my thoughts dovetailing just then with how to set about writing to you. I remember conducting myself down corridors, I remember the reflexes of light in marble halls, vaults, and stairways, but I do not at all remember queuing up and having my picture taken. Pleased, nonetheless, with my new piece of identification, with having established a traceable connection to this city, I felt at ease to turn *tout court* to the beginning of the book. With this in view I entered the Edna Barnes Salomon Room: a gallery with salmon-colored walls hung with dull portraiture—their insipidness resurfacing on faces depicted in the paintings (complexions one never knew existed)—where I stayed, inclined stiffly on a small upholstered bench, amid empty book display cabinets lined with green felt and disposed in the centre of the floor, wording and rewording my opening sentence, until I could no longer think of the book, until this mental writing had reached its salmon-pink vanishing point.

Fearn Wren

(04.14.08)

In writing this book I behave like writers who write letters about their literary work. Who use written correspondence to reflect about the work they have undertaken, to further the work, not to build rapport with their correspondents, or so much as test their reaction to the work. Or like those writers who write letters because they cannot undertake writing the book. Who make progress in their conception of a book, edge along a book, yet delay the execution of it. But in writing this book I act also like writers who make copious notes for a work they have begun or are about to begin working on. The literary man has their sights set on higher planes of creativity than the common letter can encompass; meanwhile their notepads and stationery fill up with "extra-literary" characters. There is a sense of superfluity to these productions once the literary work itself is completed. Often, by virtue of their connection with the work, such extant by-products of writing come to be seen as supplements to the work, dispositive to any real appreciation of the work. Sometimes, the "natural" order of importance between the work and the letters or notes connected with it is reversed. Sometimes, as happened here, they prove to be one and the same.

I write this work and dispatch it to your reality. On my end, writing it has from the very start been a struggle against reality: against the fixed nature of my reality and against realities that have nothing to do with me. I write the work but my reality tells me I *cannot be writing it*; I am writing but, according to reality, I *should not be writing*. And I wrote without really knowing how to write or how to continue writing, only knowing that writing had to be done. Thinking back, each note had its start in a false start. These false beginnings—some on dizzying highs, others in unplumbable lows—were the dictates of a desire for ever greater intensities in addressing you and of a crushing near-certitude of never reaching you. These non-beginnings, which you don't see, which are in themselves untraceable—each note I sent had been their composite trace (one could not erase them without erasing everything). I knew I must invent a way of addressing you, and I knew I must continue to invent new ways of address, but also that I must continue addressing you in the tried and true way. And though I left no signature, I thought of these *iters* of address as my signatures. (To give you this work, to make the gesture of giving in this work, is also to sign it over to you.) Fortunately my own restraint in extravagance makes me incapable of true extravagance. I often catch myself thinking, in relation to this work: *no stylistic embellishments, no gratuitous flourishes, only the natural marks (blemishes) of workmanship, the fingermarks of an apprentice.*

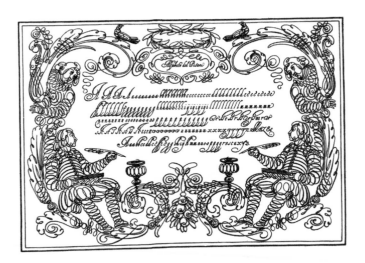

To write is to be at a distance. People are worlds apart, but the words passed between them bring them closer together, bring them into correspondence with one another. I cannot entirely forbear from thinking of this writing as an *exchange.* You have let me go on far too long where you could easily have silenced me. But our connection has not followed the rules of correspondence, born as it was out of an urge to bring myself into correspondence with you without bringing you into correspondence with me. You can dismiss it as an ultimately selfish correspondence, or you can ultimately call it selfless. But regardless of what you call it, it does not permit mutual proximity—not even an impression of it. If you want to know my take on it, my subjective take: we might not be worlds apart, yet it is as though we were. I have written on endlessly, it might seem to you—through which our distance could only grow. None of my words have brought *you* any nearer to me; they only brought out an image of you. And this image I have—I can only guess how remote it is from you (my imagination cannot possibly keep up with you!). The fuller such an image, based on surmise rather than fact, the more untrue it is likely to be. And so my desire for our extra-ordinary connection, and my denial of ordinary proximity to you, brought on an extra-ordinary distance from you. I never wished to confide in you (confidences in strangers are nothing out of the ordinary); I wished to get beyond the business of confidence, to secretly write of things anything but secret.

For these same reasons, it would not surprise me if you once felt closer to me than you do today. Without knowing a thing about me, you might have even thought me a kindred spirit. But now—now that I have made my strangerhood explicit—I feel you do not know what to make of me anymore. And could I expect you to trust anyone under a false name—this ludicrous moniker that may or may not have roots in a fondness for ferns (!) and wrens (!), ferns *and* wrens (!)? Personally, I would not trust such a person. It is entirely possible, I would think, that this individual, who not only calls themselves, but insists on calling themselves "Fearn Wren" or "F. W." for months on end, delights in pulling my leg. Can the stories told by such a person be genuine? I would suspect them all to have been fictions. But that is far from the most reprehensible thing about the entire affair. The ugliest thing about it is that you have been visited by one of those masked individuals, who refuse to reveal themselves, who probably reveal themselves as they would like to be, rather than as the monstrosities they are, and so forth . . . I can only say what I myself would think; I am not suggesting you should think any of this.

You were always free to feel the exact reverse. You may feel you know me very well now, as opposed to before. This writing may have given you a clear idea of me. (I daresay you could recognize me in the street based on the image you have formed of me!) You intuit that there's nothing in the meaning of my "name," that traceless vehicle of incognito. A total stranger has become a less total stranger, quite a familiar stranger. But for all that, on my end, these words which mediate so much of me, this masquerade which gives me so much room to maneuver—and, all the same, is the stuff of our relation—has only moved us further apart. Even if we were not exactly worlds apart, we are now very much *words apart* (some fifty thousand of them). One could estimate the distance I have put between us by counting these words as one counts footsteps. Whenever I read of you touring with your work, I instantly wish I could see it again, but in the very next instant I realize the distances involved—the spatial distance between two points on a map, the temporal distance separating your present journey from your journey some time ago, and the psychic distance separating your tour from my tarry, your remarkable mobility from my unremarkable stasis. And after every such calculation, the first distance always seems too great and the second and third not great enough. If I remain where I am, it is not because of the lack of wherewithal to go; it is simply because of images kept vivid by the effort of memory (and sundry *aide-mémoires*).

Today, as I sat down to continue this note, I thought: *I am sitting down to madness.* I have been thinking of all the writing I have here committed, of all that I had written to you—the demanding stranger that I am, the generous stranger I can be. Thinking I have temporized with a lot that, beforehand, I had really either no inkling of or never thought I could come to terms with. On a personal and technical level, this work has been gratifying to me. (I could say that it was a "gift to myself" and already be faced with the fraught question of giving, so I won't say it, and leave it at that.) But the ethical value of this work is ultimately out of my hands, as is its aesthetic value. Ultimately, my judgment of those facets would be skewed by my positive judgment of its personal and technical values. I can judge that the work is true and principled (having held fast to its principles) and that it is well-made; but I cannot trust my principles enough to judge that I have made and given you a gift, rather than simply done the work for myself and manipulated it into a gift you could not refuse (or accept either). And even if I judged that I have made you a gift of this work—that it was therefore *good*—I still wouldn't know if it was is a beautiful gift.

If it was not permitted to be a gift, what was it permitted to be? Where lies the threshold of your permissiveness? Where are the limits of your attention, patience, and receptivity to this writing act, or series of acts? (Have I not crossed every line I could cross?) Has your permission extended to my giving, or only to my writing? And if you accepted this writing as a gift, did you give it the time of day? I reach into your reality not to give and take, not to take, but to give, but have I given you anything? Do you feel gifted? Would I still consider a gift writing for which you had no use? And if my gratitude for your silence exceeded your gratitude for my gift, would the gift be gratifying to me? What are the precepts of such a gift, made over to you in parts, dedicated to you as a whole? If you have given it the time of day, did I not take as much from you in return? Must I wrap up my gift without knowing what you have made of it? I realize there are other limitations to my giving, though they haven't come up in reality. But if I stop writing, if I stop giving, will it mean I have reached my limit, or will I have merely reached the book?

The work (writing) lives, but the work (the book) dies. What do I do with the writing once it has become a book? If I give you the writing, can I then give you the book? Can I give what is mine but dead, or dead and not mine to give? I said: I am giving (giving up) my work (my writing) bit by bit. But, I said, a book must be given (up) all at once. So how exactly does one give (up) a book—without disavowing or erasing it? It was said: if one is "pregnant" with a book it must be born into the world, but stillborn. You can easily bury such books in drawers, computer folders, or libraries (*book cemeteries*). The right choice of publisher will effectively bury a book forever. And when the work is delivered and buried, one must not try to revive or revisit it, but part with it—simply let it go. One must try to breathe one's spirit into another work, one in need of a spirit.

It is now too late to abort this book. I kept (kept up) the work to continue giving it to you, or continue trying to give to you. And if I carry it through (as I have to), and attach my name to it, and it carries my name to the grave, then I have not given it up completely. Its spiritless remains will still be mine to keep and to give—but why should you care for them? I have not given the work until I have given it wholly: until I have wholly renounced it, have made it fail as a book and book experiment, and made it nothing—not even mine to give. But if I gave you what is nothing to me, if I had nothing as such to give, would you recognize that as giving? Could you take nothing for a gift? No, you would take an empty-handed gesture of giving for the vapid joke that it is. One can only take something alive and breathing, or the memory of something living and breathing, for a gift. (Just recently I wanted to present my mother with a dead moth, but realized in time how empty-handed of me that would be.) I say: to give you anything—to give you the writing and the memory of the writing—I ought to keep the book as one keeps a book: in part and to oneself. Renouncing the book would reflect *badly* on the writing, so I must not renounce it. But if I keep this book, it is also to dedicate it to you.

Alright, writing has a life of its own. Can it even be given? It was said: given bit by bit. Only bit by bit, if it's to live and to breathe. The giving of it, its piecemeal changing of hands, will soon make it whole; we will have made it to the end and, in the end, will both have it (the book, pretty much). What do we do with it? I know what I must do with it, but what could you do with it?

Instead of coming together in a body, some things have been coming apart. At and past the dissolute end of this writing lies the dissolution of the meaning of this book, and of our connection. I cannot undo this process of dissolution, nor do I wish to—for the dissolution is also a solution. One cannot erase the work of writing, but the memory of all work will sooner or later undergo erasure; bit by bit, oblivion will blanch the memory of work, pulling the work apart in our memory, whitewashing the transgressions of writing. All one will have left then will be the book. Anyhow, one can still undo the finished work: erase the physical manifestation of writing, destroy all evidence of the work, and thus the conscience of the work. Not give it up as a book: erase it before it becomes a book. If I erase it and you erase it, it will cease to exist as the would-be book that it is, the book-ward work it continues to be. If the writing will not be left undone—if, in other words, it is over and done with—together we can make it disappear. All we would have then would be our fading memories. And I would have avenged myself on this book for the miserable fate of *every book*. But I would still, I feel, take credit for the book. I would have done away with the writing, but kept my right to the work of writing. Is there another solution? Can anything *in writing* cure a writer of the vanity of the book? (Only not-writing, perhaps, can cure such vanity.) Incompleteness never fails to strike humility into a book, but is it enough? When a work is complete, when it is whole, its proud manifestation as a book becomes irresistible. One sends it to the *best* publisher, who brings it out—like the charlatan that he is, reanimating it with flimsy mechanics and pyrotechnics. Now no-one can ignore the book. To paraphrase Bachelard, the book has become permanent, an object in one's field of vision, which speaks with a monotonous authority lacking even in its author. One is fairly obliged to read it, to read one's book, to hear out its accusations and acknowledge its shortcomings. Thus the "ghost" in the book-machine "haunts" the author (its misbegetter), and only when it breaks down can the spirit of writing breathe again. We both know it (I assume you do because I do): I will let this work flow until it breaks down its potential for completeness.

I said: by writing, I am giving myself little by little, and soon I will have given myself wholly. But what did I mean when I wrote those things? Did I not simply mean: I am putting all my energies into the work and it feels sacrificial? Or have I really been giving myself up to the work? Surely this is not what I meant. I might have meant: I am giving only a part of me I can part with, the "old me" who sought distance from you. I could not have meant: I am losing myself anew. Here I note: *experiment in giving oneself cannot succeed.* Next I write: *neither succeed nor fail.* I cannot give enough of myself to write: *no more.* But I can give myself enough to write: *enough.*

One must have been crazy to try to work out the intricacies of this book. To map the ins and outs of a maze still short of completion. To get one's head around a book while one was still getting one's bearings inside it. If the writing could not resolve the book's obscurities into clarities, I hereby call for their dissolution. I repeat: *the solution of this writing (this work), taking us beyond this work (a book), is the dissolution of its meanings.* I give my permission for dissolution. I say: *the work clearing itself, erasing itself,* and I mean: *the clearing and erasing of meaning.* Best then to close the book—close it upon itself.

(04.21.08)

I am thinking of diptychs. Some diptychs confront us with life and death, resolved through prayer in a higher synthesis. The living and the dead: not antithetical to each other, only governed by divergent principles. This is underscored in the diptych through the physical divide between the panels and their attachment by hinges, whereby they close upon each other like a book. It is perhaps useless to extrapolate general principles from imaginary, nonexistent artifacts, to make predictions that may not be borne out in the execution, but I will say that a diptych pairing *monsters* and *geniuses* would have to be governed by the twin principles of darkness and light. Whether those principles are interpreted in moral and/or aesthetic terms (with one wing of the diptych overcast and the other luminous) depends on the individual executor. But monstrosity and genius are to each other as night and day. We could likewise—in a modern take on the ancient diptych writing tablet—speak of diptychs comprised of two books from the same pen, or simply of two halves of a book hinging on each other. One of them as though the work of a genius, the other, of a monster—both coeval in the mind of the author (was not Fedor Dostoevskii the modern master of this form?). But I am not thinking of any "face-off" between them; rather, I think of the faces of monstrosity and of genius as mutually complementary, if not interchangeable. Remember old Daedalus? The labyrinth, the brainchild of a great artifex, eventually imprisons him and his son, who later expires aspiring. Genius that tries to contain monstrosity itself becomes monstrous; monstrosity is no less than a flipside of genius. (A new biography of Adorno, *One Last Genius*, quotes his close friend: "Teddie is the most monstrous narcissist to be found in either the Old World or the New.") That being said, monstrosity is ubiquitous and genius scarce. An asymmetry exists between the two sides of one story: our transgression of all-too-humanness.

Genius at any price—even that of monstrosity! Solitude at the risk of monstrosity! Love at the risk of monstrosity! When I hear of someone being called a genius, straightaway I wonder about his or her monstrosity. Geniuses are often monsters we revere for their work—conversely, monsters are often geniuses from whose work we recoil in abhorrence. Works of genius are the panoplies of genius; they do not bare the stain of monstrosity (insanity, atrocity) but of deliverance from monstrosity, and one can still find in them formulae used to exorcise demons. Interestingly, the German vocable for "miscreant" and "physical malformation"—*Mißbildung*—can also be unpacked as "miseducation." And it is miseducation that seems to me the *condition of possibility* of genius. The word thus offers a positive link between genius and monstrosity. For if the objectives of education were met, the *sui generis* quality giving rise to brilliance (or madness) would be trumped by common sense and purpose.

Monstrous is not just an epithet reserved for wild or imaginary creatures, deformed bodies, or radical evil. But monstrosity is not simply *ugliness*. I have long had the impression that, despite fluctuations, the sum of ugliness has remained stable—that ugliness as such is neither in retreat nor on the advance. Ugliness is as middling a notion as is beauty, and proportionate to beauty. But monstrosity is an altogether different breed. It is a qualitative exponentiation of ugliness, and, some would say, of beauty as well. And with monstrosity, one has the impression that it has always been on the ascent (the *sublime*, inversely, has seen only indubitable decline.) Whether this is because we are less tolerant of extremes or because more extremes come into existence is not a question for which I have a ready answer. Perhaps we become increasingly sensitized to monstrosity through our exposure to the monstrous. Things that to those with thicker skins might merely seem ugly or distasteful to us seem stamped with monstrosity. Everything, from a certain angle, given enough hatred, fear, or disgust, can assume a monstrous aspect—*become* monstrous. Making do with human relationships: parents turn into monsters before our eyes all too often; lovers and ex-lovers are monstrous in more ways than one; even children show signs of nascent monstrosity. We dwell on monstrosities that are skin-deep—offensive to the senses, but inherently harmless. Meanwhile, each of us carries within him or her some nondescript "monster," a tumor that upon discovery proves malignant (when before it was benign). Piqued by our shame or another's rancor, it attacks what is most vulnerable in us: our humanness. We think with trepidation of our hidden monstrosities and fear—rightly so—that a moment's inattention will unleash them upon the world.

In the broadest sense, monstrosity is the freedom of form. We are the creators, consumers, and destroyers of monstrosity because of its power to free and shock us. (We need a "critical mass of monsters" to move art forward, is one critic's rallying cry.) If we respond to monstrosity and see in it a universal feature of modern life, we are cognizant of this proliferation of forms. The monstrous is "artificial" and "unnatural." We exclaim *Wonderful nature!* yet the forms of nature are only "wonderful" if they conform, if they do not deviate from the norms of nature. But monstrosity is the exaggeration of nature (in *lusus naturae* nature is at play). The word itself derives from *demonstration*—and monstrosity (our perception of monstrosity) does demonstrate a thing or two about our relation to the world. Most significantly, it demonstrates that we are against nature, that we tolerate only that moderate part of it, beyond which, cast out, lies the domain of monstrosity. Even genius, unless it proves itself useful to us, we cannot tolerate.

The genius and the monster, as it once seemed to me, inhabit the purest states of solitude. "The genius differs from us men in being able to endure isolation, his rank as a genius is proportionate to his strength for enduring isolation, whereas we men are constantly in need of 'the others,' the herd . . ." (Kierkegaard). Descartes had his philosophical breakthrough in a "genius incubator"; in the preamble to the second part of his *Discourse on Method*, he recalls having spent a winter day in 1619 "shut up alone in a stove-heated room" where, "having no diverting company and fortunately also no cares or passions to trouble" him, he gave himself over to his meditations. At the same time, genius and monstrosity always seemed to me the best ways out of solitude. "When I've inspired universal horror and disgust," wrote Baudelaire the Dark, "I shall have overcome solitude." I was guilty of these assumptions, based on anecdotes, at a time when I was still after the purest solitude and still leery of such (unlivable) solitude.

Recently, however, this long jettisoned complex of associations found new currency in the *monster city*. In 1942, Czeslaw Milosz wrote from occupied Warsaw about the "city as Leviathan," in whose vortex "isolated individuals struggle against isolated individuals and dream about other isolated individuals." The genius Baudelaire—a solitary walker, who, as Sartre relates, could not stand being alone even for an hour—felt most at home in the monster capital of the world. Milosz observed also "a profound bond" between cinema and the myth of the monstrous metropolis. No artistic medium captured and shaped the fusion of city and monstrosity more vividly than did film. The monster city, the labyrinthine city, unfolding night and day on celluloid, is also a work of supreme, invisible genius—whose hallmark is the absorption of monstrosity.[5] And it is also on film that the mythic status of monstrosity becomes plain; like the genius, the monster is one of the most potent modern myths.

Film shows us human monstrosity better than painting or literature—certainly more persuasively than literature—despite its debts to Goya, Bosch, and Shakespeare. In the common man it envisions a beast, in the common beast a monster. But the voyeuristic impulse pushes vision "too far." As in death and sex, so too in the monstrous the visual arts—cinema in particular—hit their ignominious rock bottom. Anatomy itself becomes monstrous; our organs are abject monstrosities exploited by a most odious and sensationalistic kind of

---

[5] Look no further than Jules Dassin's *Night and the City* for corroboration.

cinema. And just as the myth of monstrosity is given this, its richest expression in film, the ideal vehicle for the genius myth is literature. The case of Monsieur Teste, the obscure genius who never produces solid proof of his brilliance— the *fiat lux!*—the so-called work of genius—reveals genius's self-authoring hubris, built on nothing but air and captive audiences. The truth rolls off Teste's tongue in this pithy statement:

> I am at home in MYSELF, I speak my language, I hate extraordinary things. Only weak minds need them. Believe me literally: *genius* is *easy, divinity* is *easy* . . . . I mean simply—that I know how it is conceived. It is *easy.*
>
> In the past—some twenty years ago—anything above the ordinary achieved by another man was for me a personal defeat. At that time, I could see nothing but ideas stolen from me! How stupid!

Reason at the expense of sensibility, the self-absorption of reason, the vaunted excess of reason can prove captivating company—as those in its thrall readily testify. But this clarity of character is Teste's weakness, his monstrosity: without the work genius is a caricature. (Teste, of course, *is the work*, but being is not enough). The absurdity of his status reduces the genius myth to nothing, not even a *lumen obscurum.*

"The ordinary man casts a shadow in a way we do not quite understand. The man of genius casts light" (Steiner). The shadowless soul, the head like a white light bulb: the innocence of genius? The everlasting vanity of genius! "As the light grows dimmer if the candles are not trimmed, so will the world's great luminaries darken too, if no one take issue with them" (Pestalozzi). The tragic (comic!) fate of genius, which darkens not because it has to, but because everyone bathes in it. Genius burns brightly when, as Valéry says, it harbors within a false genius—a sense of imposture or failure. And Pestalozzi again: "The man who has achieved great clarity can afford deep shadows."

Monsieur Teste, composed of fragments and divesting itself of the ballast of systematicity, is a text working towards lucidity. "[O]nly those who seek nothing never run into obscurity" (Valéry). For every writer, every thinker, no matter how obscure, lucidity is the key that unlocks every door. Clarity in writing is the alchemy of thought, the hermeneutic reduction of the mind, the transmutation of verbal baseness and superfluity. The expression of genius—an expression of excess—is an expression shorn of excesses relative to its substance. Too often, however, we are duped by appearances: where verbal circumspection and a sparing style lack clarity, we presuppose great acumen: "Words, like smoke, are a sign of fire, but not the fire itself; the clearer the fire, the less smoke" (Pestalozzi). We see a trail of smoke and suppose a clear fire where there is no fire at all. As the ultimate expression of genius is silence, we suppose it to be a silence of clarity attained. But it is my uneducated guess that true genius falls silent from an *excess* of clarity—and this silence is one of madness, or death.

My memory being what I might euphemistically call *selective*, but if I were honest would call *unserviceable* (and, were I to "call a spade a spade," would call *ruined*), my reminiscences take on the quality of dreams, of made-up adventures to supplant what is almost forgotten. Memory has its *oubliettes*—chutes down which one falls into the white padded cells of fiction. Memory and oblivion (the dimness of memory, the clarity of oblivion) form a chiaroscuro continent in the mind. There is an art of memory and an art of oblivion, of unforgetting as well as forgetting. In my work as a translator, I seek accuracy in rendering pain from one language into another, for that is what I am paid to do, I am not paid to sort out accurate memories. Without their painful verifiable details, the oral and written testimonies of events now nearly seventy years back, obscure events related closely to a disaster, would be worthless—yet time and again I stumble in them upon fascinating lapses of remembrance, unknown masterpieces of oblivion. And I think: how much this man or this woman must have dreamt of a clarity that had nothing to do with understanding, but with *steering clear* of what was lodged deep in the memory—the source of suffering (the suffering source).

"[I]t is better to dream your life than to live it," wrote the young Proust, "even though living it is still dreaming it, albeit less mysteriously and less clearly, in a dark, heavy dream, like the dream diffused through the dim awareness of ruminating beasts" ["Nostalgia"]. We labor down dark and errant paths, come to many a dead-end, and when at last we reach the bright centre, it is dissolution that we have reached. If life is a labyrinth, and this labyrinth a prison, its moving centre is an "inner sun" in search of the solitary place, the *locus solus*, the man-animal monster fain to be slain. The older we become, the more we look back upon our young selves as the intrepid heroes of classical mythology, and at our present selves as the weary chroniclers of their glorious or inglorious death, saved by no god. Only yesterday, I read an interview about a community of meditating labyrinth walkers, which concluded so wonderfully that for a second I thought of joining them: "Oh, what levels of banality we can reach! There are no depths—we're only human. With your body moving, you have an advantage."

***

We are out to slay a monster. Drenched in sweat, we move along the shimmering walls of the labyrinth. We carry no weapons, only our bare hands for the closest contact with our victim. It has been a while since we lost the thread. We are moving faster. We are almost out of breath. It is high noon. No shadows. All clear.

S. D. CHROSTOWSKA is the author of *Literature on Trial: The Emergence of Critical Discourse in Germany, Poland & Russia, 1700–1800*. She teaches European Studies in the Department of Humanities at York University.

MICHAL AJVAZ, *The Golden Age.*
The Other City.
PIERRE ALBERT-BIROT, *Grabinoulor.*
YUZ ALESHKOVSKY, *Kangaroo.*
FELIPE ALFAU, *Chromos.*
Locos.
IVAN ÂNGELO, *The Celebration.*
The Tower of Glass.
ANTÓNIO LOBO ANTUNES, *Knowledge of Hell.*
The Splendor of Portugal.
ALAIN ARIAS-MISSON, *Theatre of Incest.*
JOHN ASHBERY AND JAMES SCHUYLER,
A Nest of Ninnies.
ROBERT ASHLEY, *Perfect Lives.*
GABRIELA AVIGUR-ROTEM, *Heatwave and Crazy Birds.*
DJUNA BARNES, *Ladies Almanack.*
Ryder.
JOHN BARTH, *LETTERS.*
Sabbatical.
DONALD BARTHELME, *The King.*
Paradise.
SVETISLAV BASARA, *Chinese Letter.*
MIQUEL BAUÇÀ, *The Siege in the Room.*
RENÉ BELLETTO, *Dying.*
MAREK BIEŃCZYK, *Transparency.*
ANDREI BITOV, *Pushkin House.*
ANDREJ BLATNIK, *You Do Understand.*
LOUIS PAUL BOON, *Chapel Road.*
My Little War.
Summer in Termuren.
ROGER BOYLAN, *Killoyle.*
IGNÁCIO DE LOYOLA BRANDÃO,
Anonymous Celebrity.
Zero.
BONNIE BREMSER, *Troia: Mexican Memoirs.*
CHRISTINE BROOKE-ROSE, *Amalgamemnon.*
BRIGID BROPHY, *In Transit.*
GERALD L. BRUNS, *Modern Poetry and the Idea of Language.*
GABRIELLE BURTON, *Heartbreak Hotel.*
MICHEL BUTOR, *Degrees.*
Mobile.
G. CABRERA INFANTE, *Infante's Inferno.*
Three Trapped Tigers.
JULIETA CAMPOS,
The Fear of Losing Eurydice.
ANNE CARSON, *Eros the Bittersweet.*
ORLY CASTEL-BLOOM, *Dolly City.*
LOUIS-FERDINAND CÉLINE, *Castle to Castle.*
Conversations with Professor Y.
London Bridge.
Normance.
North.
Rigadoon.
MARIE CHAIX, *The Laurels of Lake Constance.*
HUGO CHARTERIS, *The Tide Is Right.*
ERIC CHEVILLARD, *Demolishing Nisard.*
MARC CHOLODENKO, *Mordechai Schamz.*
JOSHUA COHEN, *Witz.*
EMILY HOLMES COLEMAN, *The Shutter of Snow.*
ROBERT COOVER, *A Night at the Movies.*
STANLEY CRAWFORD, *Log of the S.S. The Mrs Unguentine.*
Some Instructions to My Wife.
RENÉ CREVEL, *Putting My Foot in It.*
RALPH CUSACK, *Cadenza.*
NICHOLAS DELBANCO, *The Count of Concord.*
Sherbrookes.
NIGEL DENNIS, *Cards of Identity.*

PETER DIMOCK, *A Short Rhetoric for Leaving the Family.*
ARIEL DORFMAN, *Konfidenz.*
COLEMAN DOWELL,
Island People.
Too Much Flesh and Jabez.
ARKADII DRAGOMOSHCHENKO, *Dust.*
RIKKI DUCORNET, *The Complete Butcher's Tales.*
The Fountains of Neptune.
The Jade Cabinet.
Phosphor in Dreamland.
WILLIAM EASTLAKE, *The Bamboo Bed.*
Castle Keep.
Lyric of the Circle Heart.
JEAN ECHENOZ, *Chopin's Move.*
STANLEY ELKIN, *A Bad Man.*
Criers and Kibitzers, Kibitzers and Criers.
The Dick Gibson Show.
The Franchiser.
The Living End.
Mrs. Ted Bliss.
FRANÇOIS EMMANUEL, *Invitation to a Voyage.*
SALVADOR ESPRIU, *Ariadne in the Grotesque Labyrinth.*
LESLIE A. FIEDLER, *Love and Death in the American Novel.*
JUAN FILLOY, *Op Oloop.*
ANDY FITCH, *Pop Poetics.*
GUSTAVE FLAUBERT, *Bouvard and Pécuchet.*
KASS FLEISHER, *Talking out of School.*
FORD MADOX FORD,
The March of Literature.
JON FOSSE, *Aliss at the Fire.*
Melancholy.
MAX FRISCH, *I'm Not Stiller.*
Man in the Holocene.
CARLOS FUENTES, *Christopher Unborn.*
Distant Relations.
Terra Nostra.
Where the Air Is Clear.
TAKEHIKO FUKUNAGA, *Flowers of Grass.*
WILLIAM GADDIS, *J R.*
The Recognitions.
JANICE GALLOWAY, *Foreign Parts.*
The Trick Is to Keep Breathing.
WILLIAM H. GASS, *Cartesian Sonata and Other Novellas.*
Finding a Form.
A Temple of Texts.
The Tunnel.
Willie Masters' Lonesome Wife.
GÉRARD GAVARRY, *Hoppla! 1 2 3.*
ETIENNE GILSON,
The Arts of the Beautiful.
Forms and Substances in the Arts.
C. S. GISCOMBE, *Giscome Road.*
Here.
DOUGLAS GLOVER, *Bad News of the Heart.*
WITOLD GOMBROWICZ,
A Kind of Testament.
PAULO EMÍLIO SALES GOMES, *P's Three Women.*
GEORGI GOSPODINOV, *Natural Novel.*
JUAN GOYTISOLO, *Count Julian.*
Juan the Landless.
Makbara.
Marks of Identity.

FOR A FULL LIST OF PUBLICATIONS, VISIT:
www.dalkeyarchive.com

FOR A FULL LIST OF PUBLICATIONS, VISIT:
www.dalkeyarchive.com

SELECTED DALKEY ARCHIVE TITLES